Praise for the Novels of Lesley Kagen

The Undertaking of Tess

"A tender yet big-hearted coming-of-age story filled with heartbreak, secrets, and humorous observations of the convoluted adult world through which two young sisters must navigate."
 —Beth Hoffman, *New York Times* bestselling author of *Looking for Me*

"Heart-rending, yet humorous and filled with hope, *The Undertaking of Tess* is a rare treat from an author who truly knows how to create unforgettable characters. Readers who loved Kagen's *Whistling in the Dark* will adore Tess and Birdie in this delightful novella."
 —Sandra Kring, author of the national bestseller, *The Book of Bright Ideas*

"A bittersweet coming-of-age-in-the-fifties story that'll have you crying one minute and laughing out loud the next. Kagen's ability to capture children's deepest emotions never fails to impress."
 —Bonnie Shimko, award-winning author of *The Private Thoughts of Amelia E. Rye*

The Resurrection of Tess Blessing

"How wonderful it is to spend time inside Lesley Kagen's creative mind. In *The Resurrection of Tess Blessing*, Kagen deftly illustrates her gift for blending the serious and the funny, the light and the dark. With a touch of magical realism, she once again creates a story that's as hopeful as it is poignant. As a reader, I feel safe in her hands."
 —Diane Chamberlain, international bestselling author of *Necessary Lies*

"Kagen's talent shines in this wholly original and richly imagined story where unbearable heartache is softened with humor and a touch of magic."
 —Beth Hoffman, *New York Times* bestselling author of *Looking for Me*

"Read *The Resurrection of Tess Blessing*, but don't read it in public because it'll yank the emotions out of you. You'll laugh, you'll cry, and by the end you'll be Tess Blessing's best friend."
—Cathy Lamb, bestselling author of *What I Remember Most*

"*The Resurrection of Tess Blessing* is Lesley Kagen at her finest, magically weaving together a tale of poignant regrets, powerful aspirations, and forgotten dreams through Tess, a woman who is really a bit of each of us. By traveling this journey with Tess we are shaken, uplifted, and transformed."
—Pam Jenoff, bestselling author of *The Winter Guest*

"Confronting her own mortality, Tess Blessing, a lifelong list maker tackles the only to-do list that matters: healing fractured relationships, and empowering the children she fears she will leave behind. Poignant, funny, and searingly wise, *The Resurrection of Tess Blessing* will stay with you long after you turn the last page."
—Patry Francis, bestselling author of *The Orphans of Race Point*

"*The Resurrection of Tess Blessing* is helmed by the most interesting narrator I've read in ages. She and her gifted author, Lesley Kagen, lead us through heartbreaking, humorous, compassionate twists and turns until we find ourselves on the other side, wiser but also, appropriately, resurrected and blessed. It is a journey I was delighted to take."
—Laurie Frankel, bestselling author of *Goodbye for Now*

"I was hooked from the get go. Tess Blessing's story is quietly inspiring. With faith, hope, grace, and humor, she shows us how to keep moving forward in the face of fear, uncertainty, and pain . . . put one foot in front of the other and call in your oldest friend."
—Julia Pandl, bestselling author of *Memoir of the Sunday Brunch*

Good Graces

"*Good Graces* deftly dwells in '60s Milwaukee. Through her preteen narrator, Sally O'Malley, [Kagen] evokes the joys, sorrows, and complexities of growing up."
—*The Milwaukee Journal Sentinel*

"Kagen does a remarkable job of balancing the goofiness of being an eleven-year-old with the sinister plot elements, creating a suspenseful yarn that still retains an air of genuine innocence."
—*Publishers Weekly*

"For all the praise garnered for *Whistling in the Dark, Good Graces* more than lives up to its predecessor."
—*School Library Journal*

"A beautifully written story. . . . You will weep for and cheer on the O'Malley sisters . . . [and] immediately miss them once the last page is turned."
    —Heather Gudenkauf, *New York Times* bestselling author of *Little Mercies*

"Moving, funny, and full of unexpected delights. . . . Kagen crafts a gorgeous page-turner about love, loss, and loyalty, all told in the sparkling voices of two extraordinary sisters."
    —Caroline Leavitt, *New York Times* bestselling author of *Pictures of You*

Tomorrow River

Winner of the Wisconsin Library Association Outstanding Achievement Award

"[A] stellar third novel. . . . Kagen not only delivers a spellbinding story but also takes a deep look into the mores, values, and shams of a small Southern community in an era of change."
    —*Publishers Weekly* (starred review)

"The first-person narration is chirpy, determined, and upbeat. . . . Shenny steals the show with her brave, funny, and often disturbing patter as she tries to rescue herself and her sister from problems she won't acknowledge."
    —*Mystery Scene Magazine*

"*Tomorrow River* . . . [and] the charming genuine voice of Shenny . . . is impossible to resist."
    —*Milwaukee Magazine*

"An excellent, moving story, very well written, and one that will linger in your thoughts long after you've finished it."
—*Historical Novels Review*

"This book is packed with warmth, wit, intelligence, images savory enough to taste—and deep dark places that are all the more terrible for being surrounded by so much brightness."
—Tana French, *New York Times* bestselling author of *Broken Harbor*

Land of a Hundred Wonders

A Great Lakes Book Award Nominee

"Kagen's winsome second novel offers laughter and bittersweet sighs."
—*Publishers Weekly*

"A truly enjoyable read from cover to cover.... Miss Kagen's moving portrayal of a unique woman finding her way in a time of change will touch your heart."
—Garth Stein, *New York Times* bestselling author of *The Art of Racing in the Rain*

"I've been a Lesley Kagen fan ever since I read her beautifully rendered debut, *Whistling in the Dark*. Set against the backdrop of the small-town South of the 1970s, *Land of a Hundred Wonders* is by turns sensitive and rowdy, peopled with larger-than-life characters who are sure to make their own tender path into your heart."
—Joshilyn Jackson, *New York Times* bestselling author of *Someone Else's Love Story*

"Gibby hooks the audience from the onset and keeps our empathy throughout.... Her commentary along with a strong support cast make for a delightful historical regional investigative tale. [Gibby] is a "shoe-in" to gain reader admiration for her can-do lifestyle."
—*The Mystery Gazette*

"Lesley Kagen has crafted a story that is poignant, compelling, hilarious, real, and absolutely lovely."
—Kris Radish, author of *Gravel on the Side of the Road*

Whistling in the Dark

The Midwest Booksellers Choice Award Winner

"Kagen's debut novel sparkles with charm thanks to ten-year-old narrator Sally O'Malley, who draws readers into the story of her momentous summer in 1959. The author has an uncanny ability to visualize the world as seen by a precocious child in this unforgettable book."
—*Romantic Times Top Pick*

"Innocently wise and ultimately captivating."
—*The Milwaukee Journal Sentinel*

"I loved *Whistling in the Dark*. Living with the O'Malley sisters for the summer is an experience that no one will forget."
—*Flamingnet* TOP CHOICE Award

"One of the summer's hot reads."
—*The Chicago Tribune*

"The plot is a humdinger . . . a certifiable grade-A summer read."
—*The Capital Times*

"The loss of innocence can be as dramatic as the loss of a parent or the discovery that what's perceived to be the truth can actually be a big fat lie, as shown in Kagen's compassionate debut, a coming-of-age thriller set in Milwaukee during the summer of 1959."
—*Publishers Weekly*

"Delightful . . . gritty and smart, profane and poetic."
—*Milwaukee Magazine*

"Bittersweet and beautifully rendered, *Whistling in the Dark* is the story of two young sisters and a summer jam-packed with disillusionment and discovery. With the unrelenting optimism that only children could bring . . . these girls triumph. So does Kagen. *Whistling in the Dark* shines. Don't miss it."
—Sara Gruen, *New York Times* bestselling author of *Water for Elephants*

The Undertaking of Tess

A Novella

LESLEY KAGEN

Published by SparkPress, a BookSparks imprint,
A division of SparkPoint Studio, LLC
Tempe, Arizona, USA, 85281
www.sparkpointstudio.com

ISBN: 978-1-940716-54-1 (ebk)
ISBN: 978-1-940716-65-7 (pbk)

Cover design © Julie Metz, Ltd. / metzdesign.com
Cover photo © Trevillion Images
Author photo: Megan McCormick/Shoot the Moon
Photography
Formatting by Polgarus Studio

For the forever and always loves of my life

Casey and Riley
Charlie and Hadley

Before

To be offered the opportunity to be of service to a soul is, and always will be, a compliment of the highest order. I should've felt humbled and honored when I received the invitation from the powers that be, and I assure you, I was. Problem was, accepting a role of this magnitude was not to be undertaken lightly. This extraordinary and profound friendship is an eternal commitment, and from what I could gather from the materials I received, Theresa "Tess" Finley would essentially be up the proverbial shit creek without a paddle for most of the days she spent on Earth, which had me wondering what the odds were that I'd be successful in my endeavors. Honestly? While my heart went out to the child, I could not foresee a happy ending and I've never much cared for tragedies.

To further complicate matters, until Tess invited me into her life—God only knows when that'd occur—I'd be befriending not only her, but her younger sister, Birdie, until reinforcements showed up. Those Finley sisters were woven together so tightly that I felt certain that I, nor anybody else for that matter, would be able to separate them without damaging their essential warp.

So, on the morning I sat back to partake of Tess's Life

LESLEY KAGEN

Review—a collage similar to a Technicolor 4D movie complete with sounds and smells and tastes and touch that you don't so much observe as merge with—I admit I was doing so more out of a sense of duty than genuine interest. But, as so often happens, miracles occur when one least expects them, and as her life story unfolded, I found the reticence I'd initially felt about accepting the position lift and in its place, a sacred and everlasting love for the child settled in.

While I'm longing to give you the big picture, I'm not allowed to reveal Tess's story in its entirety at this time. After much finagling, what I *have* received is a special indulgence to share the following short clip from the days before I, her "imaginary friend," materialized in her life. I'm of the belief that once you get a glimpse of the inner workings of her heart, mind, and soul, you may come to realize, the same way I did an eternity ago, that there's just about nothing more irresistible on God's green Earth than a tale told by a scrappy, redheaded kid who's dodging the obstacles of the human race on her dash toward the finish line.

Her Life Ain't Ever Gonna Be the Same

I don't like to fish all that much and I can't swim, so you could say that I don't have any business being on Lake Michigan on August 1, 1959. No business other than love business, I mean. I'd do anything to spend time with Daddy.

We're bobbing under a sky the color that I always tell my sister is named after her—Robin's egg blue. We are also sweating a lot because this is a summer that will go down in the record books for being so hot. Usually Daddy and me fish off the banks of the cemetery pond, but today at the breakfast table he leaned over and said, "Let's beat this heat, feel the wind on our faces this afternoon. Whatta ya think, Tessie?"

I thought that I would do anything to make him happy, and it really is steamy, so I told him that sounded like a great idea before I knew that he was gonna borrow the white motorboat called *The High Life* offa Joey T, his buddy at Lonnigan's Bar on Burleigh Street, which is where Daddy works.

Maybe my kid sister would be out on the lake with us

this afternoon if Mother only woulda let us nickname her Minnow—birds of a feather and all that—but she always stays away when Daddy and me go fishing because she despises any creature with gills in a way that doesn't seem normal. Especially crappie, but who doesn't?

Because Robin Jean Finley was so small when she was born, my fisherman daddy who is a BIG jokester started calling her Minnow after we brought her home to the cemetery house, then that turned into Minnie, but when Mom told us to cut it out because we were going to give her an inferiority complex, my father thought it over and said, "How 'bout we call her Birdie? That good by you, Tessie?" Of course, Mom hated that idea too, but I gave Daddy a thumbs-up because with her fluffy hair, big eyes, and little bones, that really was a good nickname.

"What a great day to be alive and out on the lake with one of my favorite girls," Daddy says on the seat across from me in the white motorboat. He tips his head back, takes another gulp from his brown bottle of beer, and with a smile that is so blinding that it could melt snow and an I'm-about-to-tell-you-a-joke twinkle in his dark-blue eyes that are a match for mine, he also says, "Sooo . . . did you hear the one about the Polack who got stuck on the escalator, Tessie?"

I hadn't, so I tell him, "No," and then I wait for what he calls the punch line, but I guess he musta forgotten it because we've been fishing under the hot sun for so many hours. Maybe he has a little heat stroke or something because he just throws back his head and laughs, drains the rest of the bottle, and tosses it in the pile with the others on the bottom of the boat. It breaks, but that doesn't bother him, and he doesn't care that we haven't caught any fish yet either because he is an all-around happy-go-lucky person.

"You're a funny one, Tessie," he tells me, like that's about the best thing any kid of his could be.

I stay up nights trying to think up jokes that will make him laugh, but Eddie Finley is the real card in the family. Everyone in the neighborhood thinks so.

Daddy narrows his eyes at my fishing pole and says slurry, "Looks like you need another wiggler."

When he stands and reaches for the Campbell's soup can where I put the worms after digging them out of the garden this morning, he wobbles, and then he throws out his arms like he's doing an imitation of one of the Three Stooges after they slip on a banana peel. The look on his face is hilarious when he falls sideways onto the outboard motor and tumbles over the side of the boat. The splash is so big that water lands in my giggling mouth.

Daddy adores practical jokes of all kinds, but he *really* adores the ones that scare you before they make you laugh. Like when he jumps out of my and Birdie's closet, or the night he put a hunk of raw meat under our bed on Halloween, that was a good one too. That's why after he fell into the lake, I wasn't worried at all. He is an excellent swimmer who takes his jokes very, very seriously, so I'm ready for him to stay underwater longer than Houdini.

I waited and waited, but Daddy never did come bubbling up, and he didn't spurt out, "Thought I was a goner, didn't you, Tessie. *Ha . . . ha . . . ha! Gotcha!*" like he always does after a really great, scary joke.

By the time the men come roaring up in their boat, the

sun is gone. They shine a big light at me and yell, "Theresa Finley?"

I can only nod because when I try to talk, I get choked up.

"Where's your father?"

When I point over the side of the motorboat and start to cry, one of the men lifts me onto their boat and wraps a scratchy gray blanket around me even though it's still so hot. I try to take it off, but they won't let me. They tell me that I'm shocked, but I think they only want to keep me bundled up tight because they don't want to smell the throw up on my shirt and the pee in my shorts. I'm holding my breath too, so I can't blame them.

On the way back to wherever they're taking me, the one guy who is driving the blue boat and has *Stan* stamped on his shirt, shouts over his shoulder to the other guy named *Jim* who is sitting next to me, "Poor kid. Her life ain't never gonna be the same."

The hair on the back of my neck stands up when he says that because I think that maybe Stan, who I thought was kinda dumb because he has a bigger beetle brow than the prehistoric men in the downtown museum, might be right, because there's this famous saying that people can be a lot smarter than they look.

A Bird's Eye View

After someone dies, I thought it was just their body that isn't around anymore, but it's so, so much more than that. Here's my list so far:

WHAT WENT MISSING
THE SAME TIME DADDY DID

1. Bluebirds don't sing as loud.
2. Part of Birdie's mind.
3. His jokes.
4. His guarding over us.
5. His smell.
6. He won't walk me down the aisle if I get married to Charlie Garfield.

They're all bad, but #5 really got to me because there ~~is~~ was something about the way Daddy smelled that kept me coming back for more. I got to missing it so bad that I ended up sniffing every nook and cranny in the house to get a little whiff of him.

On this important morning that's two weeks after I let Daddy drown, Louise Mary Fitzgerald Finley, who is

Birdie's and my mom, is stomping around our wooden house on Keefe Avenue. She's looking for money.

There's a crash and a bang in the bathroom, and then off she goes to the kitchen to slam open cupboards and shout, "If that lazy s.o.b. had gone to work the way he was supposed to instead of going fishing, I wouldn't be . . . goddamn it all!"

She's wailing at the top of her lungs because even though she blew out twenty-nine candles on her last birthday cake she has never outgrown her tempers.

"She's got her Irish up," Daddy used to say with a smile when he came into our bedroom to escape when the two of them would be in a fight. Besides not having a big enough Friday paycheck, his hoisting a few after work bugged Mom too, which was so unfair. He was a bartender, for crissakes! Whiskey and beer were to him like . . . like gas and oil to a filling station attendant and popcorn and Jujubes to the man who owns the Tosa movie theatre.

Mom also sometimes would get mad and tell Daddy that he was winking too much at that "French slut at the bar."

Now, I don't know if cocktail waitress, Suzie LaPelt, is a slut because I'm not exactly sure what that is, but she does have *La* in her name as in *ooo . . . la . . . la* so her people definitely come from France. Major export: Evening in Paris, a perfume that is *too* popular around here. During Mass on Sundays, it stinks the church up so terrifyingly bad that when Daddy crossed himself with holy water at the front door, he'd bend down and whisper to me, "Smells like a French horror house in here." Also tongue kissing comes from that country. And same as polio came from Poland, trench mouth comes from France too because of all the trenches they got over there during the war.

Birdie and me know Suzie LaPelt pretty good because we always ~~beg~~ begged Daddy to take us with him to Lonnigan's to play the *Arabian Nights* pinball machine, drink Shirley Temple cocktails, and listen to everyone laugh at his jokes and call him, "Good-time Eddie." And on special occasions, like St. Patty's Day when everybody in the neighborhood gets three sheets to the wind, even Father Ted, especially Father Ted, Daddy would let Birdie and me entertain the customers too. We sang this song from the movie *White Christmas* with cute scarves tied around our necks. *"Sisters, sisters, there never were such devoted sisters."*

Mom barges into the living room to open up drawers in the tables and look for change under the sofa that Birdie and me are sitting on. She's having a conniption fit, but not ripping her hair out. She would never do that. It's red and very beautiful, not like mine that goes lighter in the summer and back to being darker red in the winter, but all of the time is mostly a rat's mess. She doesn't like Birdie or me to touch her hair, but especially after it's been sprayed with Aqua Net. My sister would still pat it if she was allowed, but I wouldn't 'cause I don't love her as much as Birdie does. I think our mom accidentally swallowed some of that stiffening spray and it went down her throat and into her heart.

She hasn't put on her makeup yet, but she looks very nice from her gold crucifixion necklace down. She's wearing a black dress, not her favorite color, yellow is, because it brings out the gold in her hair, but it's August 12, 1959, the day our daddy is getting pretend-buried and she has to look the part. Since she's gonna leave for church soon, I've got to put my pedal to my metal too. I came up with my most important and newest list last night that'll help keep me on track:

TO-DO LIST

1. Talk Mom into letting Birdie and me go to Daddy's pretend funeral.
2. Convince Birdie that Daddy is really dead so Mom doesn't send her to the county insane asylum.
3. If #1 and #2 don't work out, find Daddy's pretend grave in the cemetery when Mom isn't around so Birdie can say goodbye to him once and for all because seeing really is believing.
4. Decide if I should confess to the cops about murdering Daddy.

If you aren't an expert like I am on the subject of death and what happens to your body after you leave it, there are three basic things to know. Right off the bat, the deceased person pays a visit to Mr. Art Shank, the owner and undertaker of Shank's Funeral Home on Lisbon Street. He lets me sit on a high stool and watch him sometimes, not because he likes kids, but because he likes the Braves and he gets sick of listening to them play baseball on the radio with dead people who can't cheer along with him when "Hammerin'" Hank Aaron gets a home run.

After Mr. Shank pumps the stiff back up with embalming fluid that makes them nice and spongy again, he dresses them in their favorite outfit. Then he applies tan makeup to whatever skin is showing. "Not the whole body," he taught me. "That's not cost-effective." He also dabs pink rouge on their cheeks, and if they're a lady, he puts pretty eye shadow on their closed lids. When Mr. Shank is all finished sprucing the body up, he always stands back and admires his work before he places it in the satin-lined coffin that got picked out by the family. It heads over to the church after that for its funeral.

At St. Catherine's, the coffin can be left open, but only if the dead person's face wasn't messed up by a tree falling on it (Mr. Martinson) or a crazy person gave it forty whacks (Lizzie Borden) or if you get fried in the electric chair like I might for not saving Daddy because Mr. Shank is great at what he does, but he can't work miracles even if all the biddies in the parish think he can. They are always dropping off pineapple upside-down cakes, and the Italian nanas leave spaghetti and meatballs in red sauce at the funeral home's backdoor. Those old ladies also make sure to sit in the first pew and say nice and loud after every funeral things like, "My goodness, Art is so talented!"

"The Leonardo da Vinci of undertaking!"

"Why, Ruthie looks better dead than she ever did alive!"

The reason they brownnose Mr. Shank left and right is because they wanna stay on his good side so when *they* kick the bucket he doesn't fix their wagons like he did Mrs. Heinzhelder. I was listening to a baseball game with him the afternoon he "prepared" his old high school girlfriend who dumped him for Mr. Heinzhelder. The Braves were beating the pants off the Cubs, so Mr. Shank had an extra bad smile on his face when he patted on orangey face makeup, drew red lipstick way outside the lines of Mrs. Heinzhelder's mouth, and dragged her black eyebrows down to her temples. He also gave her something that she wasn't born with. An ugly mole on her cheek that he called the *coo de gra*.

When he got her right where he wanted her, the undertaker laughed like a cartoon devil when he asked me, "What do you think, Miss Finley?"

I was scared to tell him the truth because I don't want to be on his table someday and have him make me look really cruddy too. I am an excellent straight-faced liar, but I didn't think I could say that Vera Heinzhelder looked the best she ever had without cracking up, so I ended up telling him, "She . . . ahhh . . . no offense, Mr. Shank, but she . . . ummm . . . looks like a pumpkin that got dropped from a second-story window." He grinned even more devilishly and said, "Perfect!"

(This goes to prove again that honesty is the best policy, but only if you get backed into a corner and you don't have any other choice but to come clean. The more somebody knows about you, the greater danger you're in because they can use that information against you. Example: our mother.)

When the funeral is over, the coffin is lifted up by men named Paul, which is one of life's little mysteries. (What would gumshoes Stew Bailey, Jeff Spencer, and Kookie Burns from *77 Sunset Strip* think about six strong misters with the same name showing up at every funeral in black suits? They'd think it was suspicious, I bet, and worth investigating, same as me.)

After the Pauls take the casket down the aisle and out the church doors, it's driven in a black hearse that everyone follows behind in a sad parade that crawls over to Holy Cross Cemetery. It gets set six feet under in a hole that caretaker, gravedigger, and Birdie's and my friend, Mr. McGinty, digs the night before in the dark with a lantern because he feels stronger then. The crying people usually throw flowers on top of the coffin, but Mrs. Gersh threw herself because she lost her only child, a nice little girl named Eva who choked on an apple. That was over a year ago, but Mrs. Gersh still misses her daughter so much that she visits the cemetery every day come rain or shine, like the mailman. Only instead of letters, she drops off stuffed animals and cute little sweaters that she knits. She lies down and screams on top of Eva's grave, "Please let me have my baby back. Please." I always close the house windows and make sure that I'm not out on the back porch or in the cemetery around eight in the morning, which is when Mrs. Gersh shows up. I just can't take that. If Birdie or me died, our mother wouldn't howl like that, or ask God to return us. She probably wouldn't even cry if she'd already put her mascara on.

Our father's pretend funeral won't be a big production. It won't take hardly any time at all. For one thing, his coffin will be easy to carry because no matter how hard the men of the Shore Patrol looked for Daddy in Lake Michigan, he never turned up. Not on the beach. Nowheres else either. The only thing I have left of him from that day is his Swiss Army knife that he left behind in the boat. I took it up to church and had Father Ted bless it, so now it's not only lucky, it's holy lucky. I keep it on me at all times when I'm awake, and all through the night, it's under my pillow.

Birdie and me are wearing our matching red shorts and white blouses and not black this morning because even though it's really important that my sister, who wasn't there when Daddy fell out of the boat, goes to both the funeral *and* his pretend burial ceremony, it doesn't look like that's gonna happen no matter how much or how hard I beg our mother.

"Your turn, *Senorita* Birdie," I say, because I've been trying to make her feel better about Daddy being gone by doing some of my funny voices while we play her favorite game of all time—cat's cradle. "*Vaya con Dios.*"

Imitating voices is something I found out I could do one day up at school when I was making fun of Sister Raphael during choir practice. I was as surprised as everyone else was! I think it was some kind of miracle, because all of a sudden, like turning loaves into fishes, I sounded exactly like the crabby, old penguin!

A little while after that, I figured out it wasn't just her I could imitate. With some practice, I could do lots of different voices from television shows like Daffy Duck's— "Thuffering thuccotash"—and Mighty Mouse's—"Here I come to save the day." Zorro was trickier to learn than the nuns and cartoon characters, but I worked hard at it because he became Birdie's and my favorite after the Pope removed *The Cisco Kid* from the television because the Kid's horse's name was *Diablo*, which means *devil* in the language of Spain. Pope John the twenty-third doesn't care for the devil, or Spanish, he likes Latin better because it's the foreign language they teach at the seminary, which is where the boys who can't get dates go instead of high school. Since priests are the *only* people in the world who know what words like *Dominus vobiscum* mean, I hate going to Mass because it reminds me of going to a matinee movie and getting a message from Flash Gordon when I don't have my decoder ring on me.

I should talk. I don't know what the heck, "*Vaya con Dios*," means either. I only know that whenever I lower my already very deep voice for a girl, and say it like Don Diego, which is Zorro's name when he isn't wearing the black outfit and smacking his bullwhip, my sister goes into stitches and says, "Do it again, Tessie. Do it again!"

That's another one of the things I love about Birdie. Her big belly laugh. It makes me feel like at least I'm doing one thing right. Since Daddy isn't here anymore, somebody around here has got to pick up the slack because when they handed out funny bones, Mom went to the little girls' room to powder her nose.

My sister at least *tries* to be funny, but she can't tell a joke, not even a simple one. She'll say, "Knock . . . knock." And then I'll say, like you're supposed to, "Who's there?" And then she'll say, "Birdie." And then I'll say, "Birdie who?" Then she'll say, "It's me, Tessie. Let me in."

See what I mean? That's why I had to work hard on a very good fake laugh for two days. I don't want her feelings to get hurt because they can very easily. Just like her outsides, Birdie's heart is very delicate.

Still giggling a little, she wiggles the bakery string that she's got looped around her fingers in my face. "Your turn." I don't like this game. (I call it crap's cradle in my brain.) I'm only playing it because I love her, and I can erase some of my sins by making a sacrifice, which this is, because Birdie's gonna beat me, she always does. She's not good at telling time or reading or figuring things out, but she's really, really great at card games and she is a goddamn cat's cradle genius!

"Theresa!" Mom yells outta her bedroom. She never calls me Tess, or Tessie, like ~~Daddy~~ Birdie does. She thinks nicknames are low class. "Get in here."

"That's okay. I give up. You win!" I say to my sister after she drops her hands and the cradle collapses in her lap 'cause the sound of our mother's bossy voice can make whatever is going on in Birdie's head come to a grinding halt. "Be right back for round two."

I'm not sure Birdie hears me though. Besides "tweetheart," Daddy called her his "little dreamboat"— another great nickname because she can drift off, and sometimes it really does seem like she falls asleep in the middle of things.

She's also very sweet with blah-brown hair, pale-blue eyes, a baby-talking voice, and her ears lie close to her skull, but I don't want to paint too rosy of a picture. She does have some *not* so good points too. Birdie is VERY high strung. If you stand next to her for too long, you can feel her vibrate like the tuning fork in music class. She also picks at scabs, and she can be more stubborn than a blood stain. Once she gets something locked into her mind nothing, and I mean *nothing*, me or anybody else says will open it back up again. Our mother says Birdie is also, "Thick as a brick," because she weighed next to nothing when she was born and her brain got short-changed. Besides being dumb, she also thinks that my sister might be, like they say in the cowboy movies at the Tosa Theatre when one of the prospectors starts acting weird, "Touched in the head."

"Theresa Marie!" our mother hollers again. "Are you deaf?"

"Keep the string warm, I'll be right back, my little dreamboat," I tell Birdie, but she doesn't answer me again because she really is going more drifty by the second. She wet the bed last night.

The Hungarians

In the bedroom that belongs to only her now, our mother is sitting on the ~~throne~~ stool in front of her vanity mirror, her all-time favorite spot.

My eyes go straight to where there should be a picture of her and Daddy next to all the beauty potions. Where'd it go? They were at the Milky Way Drive-in. She was sitting on the hood of a jalopy and our father was looking up at her the way he always ~~does~~ did. Like she was a four-leaf clover. Mom is staring at him with a lucky look too, which is so hard to believe that I bet she paid to have the picture guy at Dalinsky's Drugs doctor it up.

"You rang, madam?" I ask my mother in my excellent Maynard G. Krebs beatnik voice.

"Knock it off," she says without taking her eyes off herself. They are a very unusual blue, somewhere between my navy ones and Birdie's light ones. Hers are shot with blood today. I've never actually seen her cry in person, but I knew she did last night because Birdie and me could hear her through the wall that separates our bedroom from hers. I think she was crying because she couldn't fall asleep without Daddy. Him not cuddling her? I can see how that would set her off because I can't drift off to sleep unless I feel my sister's breath blowing like a summer breeze on the back of my neck. I've been wondering for awhile if I didn't wash the dirt off it for a whole week, could I sprinkle a few seeds back there, let my sweat water them, and wear my hair in a ponytail so they'd get some sunlight, would they grow into a little sweet-smelling pink peony bush? That seems like that would work, that's all the ingredients you need to grow something, but I'm gonna ask the best gardener I know, our gammy, the next time I see her, which could be today at Daddy's pretend funeral, if our mother would only play ball.

When she says to me like she read my mind, "I want you to call your grandmother," my knees almost give out and my tummy shrinks into a medicine ball. The idea that she could ESP my thoughts is one of the most sickening things I can think of.

"Ahhh . . . how come?" I ask, hoping she doesn't say, 'So you can ask her about planting pink peonies on the back of your dirty neck so you and your sister could fall asleep every night breathing in one of the best smells in the entire world, you idiot.'

Mom doesn't say that, but what she *does* say is almost as scary, "Because I told you to, and I'm the boss now." She goes back to gliding on her bright-red lipstick that makes her pale skin and black A-line dress with the white collar really stand out.

"What do you want me to say to Gammy?" I ask her.

"Tell her that you and your sister are starving."

Now, I'm not against lying, it really is one of my best qualities next to my funny voices, but I don't like doing it to people I adore unless it's an emergency, which this isn't.

Mom must've forgotten about the boatload of food the ladies from church brought over. She wouldn't let me answer the door because we aren't, "Charity cases, for crissake," so they left their tuna-noodle casseroles and beef stews on the front porch alongside the million containers of goulash that got delivered by the other ladies who wear babushkas to church instead of hats or scarves. Birdie and me ate the goulashes already because we feel really bad for the fattest people in the parish. It's sad, really. No matter how much or how often those babushka-wearing ladies eat, they stay starving, which is why their neighborhood nickname is, "The Hungarians."

Mom is brushing her luxurious hair with the silver brush and staring at me in the mirror. "Tell your grandmother that we ran out of grocery money." She lined her eyes in black pencil and she stroked the lids with shadow made by the Revlon company. Dusky Blue is her favorite, same as Mr. Shank's, which can't be a coincidence. "Ask her to bring some cash to the funeral."

One of the reasons she wants me to call Gammy is because Mom *really* loves money and she doesn't have any other family she can ask for some. You think she'd feel sorrier for Birdie and me because she must understand at least a little how we're feeling. Her father died just like ours did, but not from drowning in a lake, from being a hero in the war. And her mother passed on a few years ago too from having something bad in her bladder or falling off a ladder, one of those two things. Mom won't talk about it. She had a big brother for awhile named Virgil, but he ran off when he was sixteen to join the Navy and nobody ever heard from him again. If there is anybody else in her family like cousins or aunts and such, I never heard.

The other reason Mom wants me to call Gammy is because she would never get what she wants if *she* called. Our grandmother loves Birdie and me, but not her. She calls our mother behind her back, "The little trollop." This doesn't sound so bad to me, but Boppa told me that it's a huge insult if your people come from where they do—England. Chief exports: tea, Sherlock Holmes, and flowers.

I'll call our gammy, but just to tell her I love her, and ask her the question I had about growing pink peonies on the back of my neck. I won't let my mother know that I didn't ask that sweet old lady for grocery money because that would make her mad and I have to keep the peace around here. I'll tell her there was no answer.

"Sure, okay, I'll call Gammy right away and tell her to bring some dough to the funeral, but before I do that . . . ah. . . ." I *have* to try to convince her one more time. For my little sister's sake. She really *needs* to get to Daddy's pretend funeral. Even though he won't be inside the casket, just seeing it, and hearing everyone blubber, would help Birdie understand the truth. "Please . . . if you don't want us at church, could you at least let us go to the burial?" My sister could watch the box get lowered into the hole in the poor person's part of the cemetery. She could press her lips against the gravestone that the veterans donated that would have his birthday and deathday engraved in it. That would be a huge help!

Mom says, "You may have had your father wrapped around your little finger, Theresa, but when *I* say no, I mean no."

"But *why* can't we go? What's the reason?"

She spins around to face me with the same look she gets on her face when she cleans leftovers out of the fridge. "You know what Mrs. Klement and all the other ladies in the Pagan Baby Society call you and Robin Jean?"

Mrs. Gertrude Klement is our repulsive next-door neighbor. She's my number-one enemy, and a big muckety-muck at St. Catherine's. She's also on one of my *other* lists.

MY SHIT LIST

1. ~~Dennis Patrick.~~
2. The greasy man who tries to peek in the gas station bathroom window when you gotta stop to pee because you can't make it home from the Tosa Theatre after you drink a large root beer.
3. Mrs. Gertrude Klement.
4. Mom.
5. Jenny Radtke.

Because I'm not ashamed of the neighborhood nickname—those pagan ladies are nothing more than a bunch of ignorant Amoses—I stick out my chest and answer my mother, "They probably call us the Finley *ghouls*." Their kids *used* to call us that too instead of the Finley *girls*. Ha . . . ha . . . ha. They'd act like zombies, and shuffle-yell at Birdie and me at recess until I lost my temper and showed them what Daddy taught me in the storage room at Lonnigan's Bar. I know how to throw a punch, because he was not only a great father, he was a great fighter. He won trophies when he boxed at The Eagle Ballroom when he was younger in the Golden Gloves contest. "Keep moving. Never let 'em get you against the ropes, kiddo," was one of his best tips. "And I don't care how bad you're bleeding or how much you wanna quit a fight, a Finley never, ever throws in the towel."

Mom repeats disgusted, "The Finley *ghouls*," and smacks her silver hairbrush down on the vanity like this is her courtroom and it's a gavel. "I rest my case."

That'll be the day.

She hounds me and Birdie all the time about being too "morbid." One of the ways she thinks we could be livelier is by getting a different hobby like baton twirling or hula hooping. Why can't she see that *our* hobby isn't just some stupid fad that is in today, out tomorrow. Death has been around forever, and it's not going anywhere anytime soon.

All the nuns ever talk about in catechism class is dying, and how you better follow their rules and the Ten Commandments, or else you will get stoned or smitten and go to hell. Those are God's two favorite ways to do away with people who don't turn their book reports in on time, which is also a sin, but from what I can tell, just about everything is. Kids throw stones at each other all the time, so I understood what stoning was, but I wasn't sure what *smitten* meant. Since priests and sisters pinch your ear really hard if you ask too many questions, I had to figure that out on my own. *Smitten* is a combination of two words. It means that if you don't buckle under, God will get ticked off and strangle you with a mitten. Your tongue would pop out of your head and you would drool, so that doesn't sound like a good way to go. Wet wool really stinks.

Birdie and me talk a lot about the best way to die. For a while, she thought hanging herself from a tree like they do to the horse thieves in the cowboy movies wouldn't be that bad, until I brought up that she doesn't like to have tight things around her neck. So now she thinks sticking her head in Mrs. Carmody's oven would be the best way to do away with herself because that lady wins prizes for her pies. Smelling warm cherries or apples and cinnamon instead of getting a bad rope burn before Birdie fell to sleep forever *would* be much better, so I agreed with her. Since I love thunderstorms, the same way our daddy did, I think going to the middle of the cemetery during a terrible storm so I could get struck by lightning would be great. (And, Mr. Shank I'm sure would agree, very cost-effective.)

But that's just a fun game Birdie and me play, we wouldn't really suicide ourselves. No matter how heartbroken you are, Catholics aren't supposed to. The priests got so mad at Mrs. Garfield when she closed the garage doors and left her car motor running that they wouldn't even let her body get buried in Holy Cross Cemetery, which was really crummy of them. Her son, Jasper, who I call Charlie because his real name makes him sound like he's the twin brother of Casper the Ghost—I like him. A lot. Even if he doesn't have hair. Since Charlie lives on the other side of evil Mrs. Klement, to visit his dead mother all he'd have to do is climb the black iron cemetery fence the same way Birdie and me do whenever we want to hang out over there. I don't know where they ended up burying his mom, he doesn't like to talk about it, but I know he has to take the #11 bus to bring her daffodils and that none of his sisters or brothers go with him because they are ashamed of their mother for killing herself. Charlie isn't, he still loves her, so that makes me like him even more.

And it's not just in the Bible that dying is so popular! It's all over the television shows. Unless someone gets poisoned or shot in the stomach, private detectives can't solve the crimes so they'd be out of a job!

In the matinee movies, death is VERY big too. In every monster movie ever made—*The Blob* or *The Thing*, for example—a lot of dying goes on. Even Mr. Walt Disney loves death. Look at what happened to Bambi's mother, for godssakes!

I check the clock next to Mom's bed and talk quick because time is running out. "I'm alright to stay home this morning, but Robin Jean really, really *needs* to go with you to Daddy's funeral because she doesn't believe that. . . ."

Uh-oh.

Mom stops powdering her freckled nose and says in a voice that's so cold that I check for frost on the vanity mirror, "Robin Jean doesn't believe *what*?"

This bothers me so much. Not taking my word on something is not Birdie's regular personality. She usually believes everything I tell her.

I laugh real fast and tell our mother, "Ahhh . . . never mind, it's dumb," because I gotta keep that secret between my sister and me. That would be dangerous information for our mother to have. "You know, Birdie."

I feel bad about razzing my sister, but I need to get Mom off this subject before she gets it in her head to give Birdie the third degree. My sister is not strong like me. One of the things I practice when I can't sleep at night is imitating a brick wall, but Birdie will cave in to our mother's torture faster than you can say Rumpelstiltskin.

"Oh, I just love your earrings, by the way!" I say, because showering her with compliments works most of the time when I need to make her forget what she was talking about in the first place. "They match your eyes perfectly!"

The pink powder pad she's pressing against her chin moves along with her lips when she says, "Try all you want, Theresa, but you're not going to get around me the way you could your father. Funerals are for grown-ups."

Unless you're the dead kid.

Birdie and I have watched tons of burials through the fence over the years, and a lot of them are small caskets because we can die of polio, but also scarlet fever can get us, and the German measles can attack the kids whose last names are Holzman or Kleinman, anything that ends in m-a-n. Ringworm can kill you too, so I'm a little worried about Charlie because that's why he's bald. He doesn't seem bothered that worms ate all his hair, but getting something like that would make me suspicious about my scalp for the rest of my life. Your head is a big part of your body, landmass wise. Since geography is one of my three best subjects in school, I know what I'm talking about. I get A's in reading and spelling too. I also love to sing in the choir even though I have to do alto with the boys because of my very low voice that Tommy Aglietti kept telling everybody, "Finley sounds just like Froggy the Gremlin. Plunk your magic twanger, Finley," until I punched him in the bread box. I hate arithmetic. And catechism. And Tommy Aglietti stinks too, and not only because his family eats a lot of this Wop spice called garlic to keep safe from vampires.

Kids can get murdered too.

There was a lot of gossip going around the neighborhood earlier this summer about the dead body of a little girl getting found next to the Washington Park lagoon, which is not that far away from us. Maybe ten minutes. There was another dead girl the summer before that too, I think, I wouldn't swear to it. I didn't know the girl they found murdered next to the lagoon because she didn't go to St. Catherine's, a.k.a. St. Kate's, she went to Mother of Good Hope, but our mother knew the mother of Sara Heinemann because they both went to Washington High School. When Mom read Birdie and me the story outta the newspaper, she didn't seem too worried that we might get murdered too. She just folded the *Sentinel* up and said, "Don't take any candy from strangers, Robin Jean." That was good advice, for a change, because Birdie has a HUGE sweet tooth and will eat every candy that was ever created. If Jack the Ribber offered her black licorice, hard to believe, but she'd take it.

Kids also get run over by cars, which is a good thing to remind my mother of.

"You let us go to Dennis Patrick's funeral." He was a sixth grader at our school who got flattened by a Rambler on Appleton Avenue. The nuns at St. Kate's made the whole school attend his funeral. They forced us to file past the casket and tell him something nice. If it was up to us, Birdie and me would laugh and give him the thumbs up. We had to practice looking sad for a whole half hour in the bathroom mirror the night before so when it was our turn to lean down and whisper something into Dennis Patrick's dead ear—I'm sorry to have to report that Mr. Skank did a really nice job on covering the tire tracks—no more nasty rumors would get started about the "Finley ghouls." What we ended up telling Dennis was, "Good riddance to bad rubbish, you little shit," but with really sad looks on our faces. We were glad that the bully who knocked your mouth into the bubbler and would trip you on your way to the bathroom, and one time ambushed me in the alley and tried to pull off my Friday undies, was deader than a doornail. If Birdie, who is fragile, but also wiry, hadn't snuck up and hit that moron with a rock between his shoulder blades, he woulda . . . he woulda . . . I don't know what he woulda done. Why'd he want my Friday undies so bad? Not to give them to Goodwill the way Mom gave away Daddy's things, that's for sure. That kid didn't have a charitable bone in his body even before it got run over.

My mother closes her gold compact with a snap and says, "Hmmm. . . . I did allow you to go to the Patrick kid's funeral, didn't I. Good point." She's tapping her chin like she's thinking over what I said and might let Birdie and me go with her after all, but I am no patsy. I don't let my hope get up very often that she's about to do something nice, not like my sister does. Mom is just putting out one of her traps. I know this because if you watch somebody long enough, you can pick up all their little tricks. She arches her right eyebrow when she's about to spring something on me. "But you and your sister are *not*, I repeat, *not* going to your father's funeral, Theresa. Period."

She gets busy then pulling on the black stockings with the seams past her pretty right knee. "Goddamn it," she says. A runner sprang up around her ankle and raced up her calf. "Now see what you made me do?!"

She stands up quick and takes a giant step toward me. I duck because I think she's gonna give me one of her "love taps," but she reaches over my shoulder and yanks open the top drawer of her bureau where she keeps her unmentionables.

I tell her, "I'm sorry. I'll go call Gammy for money," and then, since Daddy's not here anymore to tell her how beautiful she is and somebody has to, I add on as I back outta the room, "You remind me so much of Greta Garbo," because she's a sucker for movie star compliments. Not all of 'em are true, but that one happens to fit her to a T. That actress always *vants* to be left alone too.

I Gotta Get to the Bottom of This Once and for All

TO-DO LIST

1. ~~Talk Mom into letting Birdie and me go to Daddy's pretend funeral.~~
2. Convince Birdie that Daddy really *is* dead so Mom won't send her to the county insane asylum.
3. If #1 and #2 don't work out, find Daddy's pretend grave in the cemetery when Mom isn't around so Birdie can say goodbye to him once and for all because seeing really is believing.
4. Decide if I should confess to the cops about murdering Daddy.

Just because Mom already drove off in the woody looking sadly beautiful, that doesn't mean that Birdie and me absolutely can't go to Daddy's pretend funeral. That's why I crossed out #1 in pencil and not ink.

St. Kate's is only two blocks down and the Finley sisters are fast runners—you gotta be around here. We wouldn't have to be careful about somebody seeing us on our way over there because EVERYBODY will be in those pews crying. Even Mrs. Gertrude Klement, our spying next-door neighbor wouldn't be around to watch my every move and report it back to our mother. Once we got to the church, we'd have to be more careful. We could crawl on our tummies through the big doors like Apaches scouting out a wagon train. I love Indians. Chief exports: moccasins, pemmican, and scalps. I always root for them in the Western movies. They not only dress great, they're really smart, and own tomahawks, which I'd love to get for a birthday present this year. Apaches wouldn't be caught dead wearing red shorts when they're trying to bushwhack pioneers because that's a color that sticks out, so Birdie and me would have to change into our tan shorts. That way we could stay in a way-back pew that we'd blend into so nobody'd notice us. When it was all over, we'd leave the same way we came. Belly-crawling-Indian style.

That's a good plan, but not perfect, because in our neighborhood, the famous saying, "Mind your own beeswax," is *never* true. Everybody is always buzzing around, watching each other, just waiting for someone to slip up. So no matter how sneaky my sister and me were, one of the busybodies, who are always looking to gather gossip to pass around with their cream-filled coffee cake at the next Pagan Baby Society meeting, might get a bead on us. The news that the poor, fatherless Finley ghouls were at the pretend funeral would spread faster than a prairie fire. Our mother would have one of her temper tantrums. Not in church, of course. She cares too much what people think about her to do that. She'd wait until everyone went back to crying in their hankies before she lifted the veil on her black pill box hat and gave us a look that'd let Birdie and me know that as soon as she got home she'd try her hardest to make us sorry for being born. Daddy believed in sparing the child, but she believes in the belt, and sending us to bed without supper—a bad one for Birdie who doesn't eat like her namesake. She eats like a pirate. Or maybe Mom will stop talking to us, which I don't mind at all, but that's hard on my sister too. And the other night when we didn't take out the garbage fast enough, she told us she'd had it up to here and put us in the woody wagon and dropped us off at the park and didn't come back for an hour. Birdie is very ascared of the dark.

I'd put up with one of our her dumb punishments if seeing Daddy's casket would help my sister, but I'm not sure a kid who reminds me sometimes of a stack of Pick-Up Sticks that might come tumbling down with one bad pull—could handle that right now on top of Daddy being dead.

Forgetting about the church funeral altogether and going straight to the cemetery might be a brighter idea. We could climb the black iron fence and hide behind mausoleums until we got close enough for a good look. But there's a risky part in that plan too. Sometimes Birdie can be as unpredictable as Mom, but in a different way. Not mean. I can't count on my sister not to do something really weird. Like all of a sudden decide to run out from where we're hiding yelling, "Hello! Hello everybody!" and our mother would blow a gasket.

Nuts.

I hate to let Daddy down and throw in the towel, but we learned in school that the state of Wisconsin—chief exports: cheese and milk—has the motto *Forward*, and I try to remember that at all times. So since #1 on my TO-DO LIST is now dead in the water, I've got to get busy working hard on #2 this morning: Convince Birdie that Daddy is really dead so Mom doesn't send her to the county insane asylum.

I thought at first it'd be easy to talk my sister into the truth, but it's turning out to be much harder than I thought because I forgot to figure in her stubborn streak. She seemed like she believed me when we first talked about how Daddy died the night the men brought me home after they found me in the boat on Lake Michigan. She cried and cried in my lap, and even gagged when I told her how when he fell into the lake some of the water splashed into my mouth, but now the Finley sisters have parted on this subject like the Red Sea. Birdie is 100% positive that our father is still alive and I gotta get to the bottom of this once and for all before she blows it and tells our mother.

Death Makes You Smarter and Can Taste Great Too

Even on a hot, calm day like this one, if you sit on the back porch of our house and you turn your face to the left, toward Lake Michigan, even though it's miles and miles away from where we live, you can catch a whisper of wind on your cheek. I know it's dumb, but I like to pretend that a part of Daddy is in that breeze. He smelled fishy alotta the time too.

I told Birdie we should come out here to get cooler after Mother left, and that we could play a game and I'd paint her toenails the pretty shell pink that're the same as Mom's because she wants to be just like her, and that only goes to show again how her brain isn't working right. But the *real* reason we're out on the back porch is because Holy Cross backs up into the yard of our house. Even though the cemetery is gigantic and does a great business, I've got my fingers crossed that we might get lucky and see Daddy's fake funeral through the iron fence with the spears on top that circles the cemetery like a black necklace.

Birdie and me always like to look at the flowers,

pictures, and presents that people leave on the graves of the ones who left them behind. One lady who works at Melman's Hardware store on Vliet Street, I think her name is Evelyn, she places a heart-shaped box once a month on the grave of a man named Leonard Lindley. Born April 23, 1920 – Died March 6, 1949. Mr. Lindley used to be a plumber until he and his wife got burned alive in a house fire. What Birdie and me learned from his death is that it's not a good idea to smoke in bed, and that Mr. Russell Stover makes excellent chocolate-covered cherries.

See how educational and delicious death can be? Much more than what you can learn at school if you don't count geography, which I *need* to know when Birdie and me run away someday. We don't wanna wander around like Hansel and Gretel, who had to be the two biggest *dummkopfs* in all of Germany—chief exports: warm potato salad and war. For crissake, what kind of stupid *schlemiels* go for a walk in a place called, "The Black Forest?" That's just asking for something Grimm to happen! (That's a joke I made up. Daddy loved it.)

Reading is also an important subject at school. Like the sign on the wall at the Finney Library reminds you whenever you check books out: *Knowledge is power.*

That's a famous saying that I only agree with a little. Knowing stuff *is* good, but there is nothing as powerful in the whole world as being lucky. Since Birdie and me have never found a four-leaf clover no matter how hard we look, I decide that instead of going over the cemetery fence to look for the funeral, we better stay put right where we are. I'll cross out #1 with my ballpoint pen instead of pencil soon as I get a chance.

Feeling like a broken record, I tell my sister, "Daddy's dead."

"Your turn," she says. "No, he's not."

Clue and checkers are much better games, but we're playing Candy Land. It's her favorite board game because it doesn't have reading or thinking, and it's also about her favorite food group. I am the blue piece. She's yellow, same as always.

"Yeah, he really is dead, Bird."

"Is not."

That's when it hits me how dumb I've been. Stupid. Stupid. Stupid. I got so caught up explaining to her that Daddy *is* gone, that I forgot to ask an important question that could solve this problem in a snap. I really have to work on grilling people. I should put that on a future TO-DO LIST.

"Okay," I tell my sister, "if you don't believe that Daddy is at the bottom of the lake then where is he?"

"Boca Raton."

Well, that stopped me on my hop over to the Candy Cane Forest. "Boca . . . what?"

"Boca *Raton*," Birdie says like I'm deaf and dumb. "It's a city."

"Oh, yeah?" I have never heard of it and I know a lot more cities and states and capitals and exports than she ever will. "Where is it?"

"Florida."

Chief exports: oranges and fourth runner-up in last year's Miss America show.

I'm gonna win that bathing-beauty contest someday. When I get older, and grow big bellows. Seems like being pointy in the chest is really important in all of life, not only if you wanna wear that crown. Boys and men like bellows to be big under a tight sweater or your school uniform. The Italians seem to grow them larger and faster than anybody else. Example: Mary Sarducci. Even though she's only going into the sixth grade, hers are already so huge that her hand sticks out about a foot when she's pledging the allegiance to the flag. But large bellows aren't the only important part of winning, having a talent is a big deal too. I'm planning to sing *My Favorite Things* because it's Birdie's favorite tune on the record that Mom plays on the hi-fi. I might throw in a little yodeling like Shirley Temple does in *Heidi* because who isn't in love with *her*? My mother, who can always guess the winner of the show when we watch it on TV, told me, "I wouldn't get my hopes up if I were you, Theresa. You take after your father's side of the family." She's right. My ears do stick out like Daddy's, but on the upside, his mom, my and Birdie's gammy, has bellows the size of feather pillows, so I'll probably inherit those too. As soon as the judges get a load of them, they'll forget all about my ears. But probably the best thing I'll have going for me is that you have to be able to talk to Mr. Bert Parks and not sound stupid and even my mother agrees that I've got a smart mouth.

I draw another card out of the Candy Land deck and tell Birdie, "I never heard of Boca Raton being in Florida." The only city I ever heard of is Miami Beach. "You sure 'bout that?"

"A hundred percent positive."

I love her to death, I would take a bullet for her or

jump off a cliff for her, even eat liver and onions for her, but Birdie makes stuff up a lot of the time, or borrows ideas from someone else that she tries to pass off as her own. She told me once that she invented aluminum foil. But there was something different in the way she said, "Boca Raton." She seemed really sure of herself.

I reach across the board and swipe off the beads that have popped up on the side of her little ski-jump nose with the Kleenex I always keep in my pocket for when she picks scabs or gets too sweaty. "Did you learn about Boca Raton at school?"

She moves to the next yellow square and says, "Nope," with a teasing smile. She likes it when she thinks she knows something that I don't. Loves lording it over me, really, because her being smarter than me doesn't happen very often, in fact, just about never. "I heard about it at Dalinsky's. There's a picture postcard taped on the side of the cash register and the man on the front of it is Daddy! He's holding up a huge silver fish with a pointy nose and wearing a blue shirt. Mister Dalinsky told me it says, "Greetings from Boca Raton! Wish you were here!"

Oh, boy.

I slowly draw another card to give myself some time to think. It's purple, so I kiss it because it's my favorite color. Most Catholics love it because it stands for penance, which is really popular around here.

"So . . . ," I say as I move my piece, "lemme get this straight. You think that Daddy is on a postcard that's sticking to the cash register at the drug store and . . . and that he's sending you a secret message that he wishes you were in Boca Raton with him?"

The pigtails I put into Birdie's hair this morning bob up and down many times.

That's a weird thing to think, but I am not completely thrown like some people would be if they heard her say something like that because I'm her sister. Nobody knows the Bird like I do.

The reason she believes this is because the both of us love mystery stories of all kinds, but especially Nancy Drew ones, and that girl sleuth is always finding secret messages in clocks and under rocks. I read the books out loud to Birdie because it can take a whole day of listening to her sounding out words to get past one page of a story and that is very annoying. It is safe to say that she will not be a librarian when we grow up. *If* we grow up, that seems so far-fetched. I would not be surprised at all if the both of us end up becoming private detectives, also known as private dicks in *True Detective* that they sell in the rack at Dalinksy's next to the *Look* magazines. (The drug store is another place where I learned about the importance of big bellows. There is always a broad who fills out a sweater so nicely that the private detective is happy to take on her case for free.) I will be the brains of the Finley Sisters Detective Agency; Birdie'll be more like Suzanne who answers the phone on *77 Sunset Strip* and is also very cute.

My sister draws another card out of the pile. Green is the Irish's favorite color, so Birdie and me only half-love it because the other part of us is English.

"They looked really hard for three days and they didn't find Daddy in the lake," Birdie says very cocky.

"Yeah, but just because they didn't find him," I say,

"that doesn't mean that he isn't down there."

"Doesn't mean that he is, either."

"But . . . that doesn't make sense, Bird. If he *is* still alive, after he fell outta the boat, why didn't he just get back in? And why didn't he just come home?"

"He wanted to, but he couldn't because he got am . . . am . . . am—"

"His arms got amputated?"

She flaps hers up and down. She does that sometimes when she gets frustrated. "He didn't get back in the boat with you because he got am . . . am . . . amnesia."

Double, oh, boy.

This is an even kookier idea, but I'm a little relieved she believes this. I thought she was gonna say something much, much worse. Like the reason Daddy didn't get back in the boat after he fell out was because he was so mad at me for not diving in after him that he just said the hell with that ungrateful brat and swam away.

No one has said anything to me yet. Not the cops. Not even Mom, but I bet she's thinking it. Even Birdie has to be wondering why after Daddy fell overboard, I just sat in the white motorboat and laughed my butt off the whole time he was drowning because I wonder that too.

If I had to do it over again, I woulda dove in and tried to save him even though I can't swim. That might've been for the best, after all. Daddy and me paying a visit to Davy Jones locker together. But what would happen to Birdie if I wasn't around to protect her? To keep our mother from knowing that she's going even weirder? She'd call the men in the white jackets to take my sister away, that's what'd happen.

Lately, I've been suspecting that Mom would like to do that to me too because she's been giving me ~~funny~~ funnier looks. Just because I can't eat sloppy joes and chipped beef on toast points anymore because they were Daddy's favorite. And when she made me go to the grocery store with her last week and I saw a bottle of milk, which he also loved with a little whiskey stirred in before bedtime, I did something that I *never* do in front of her. I started to cry, which turns her stomach, so I sucked back the tears, held my breath, and closed my eyes, but the sadness came bursting out anyway. I threw it up in aisle four.

Mom made me wait for her out in the Red Owl lot, and after she came out the doors with the bags in her arms and loaded them into the woody, she was so ticked off all the way home. Even though I told her I was sorry four times. She said, "Are you? Do you even have a conscience? Mrs. Klement told me that she saw you stealing something from the Five and Dime yesterday." I told her, "I'm innocent!" which was the truth because what I took wasn't for me, it was a birthday present for Birdie, so it was more like being Robin Hood robbing from the rich and giving to the poor. "Gert made that up! You know how hard her arteries are going!" My mother snorted, and sucked so hard on her L&M cigarette that her cheeks caved in, but every so often I'd catch her giving me not a mad look, but a jumpy sideways look through the cloud of smoke. Like maybe she didn't have Bonnie Parker on her hands, but a *Bad Seed*. I'd betcha a dollar that as soon as we got home she'd telephone the school and tell Sister Raphael to call off Friday spelling bees when school starts up just in case I get it into my head to kill one of the kids for their winning medal—probably the girl who sits in front of me, Jenny Radtke. Just because I stare at the back of her perfect blond page boy and try to set it on fire with my eyeballs because she is such a little ass-kisser who doesn't deserve such beautiful hair, or to win that goddamn spelling bee every single Friday, that doesn't mean I'd murder her. After letting Daddy die, I promised myself I wouldn't murder anyone ever again unless they were trying to hurt Birdie.

While my sister is moving around the Candy Land board (she's cheating), I take my TO-DO LIST out of my pocket and stare at #4: Decide if I should confess to the cops about murdering Daddy.

I'm pretty sure that's what my conscience wants me to do. Walk over to the 51st Street Station House and turn myself in. But now that I've really thought if over, after I confessed and they took me away to prison and electrocuted me, that would be the same as me drowning when I tried to save Daddy. I wouldn't be fried for longer than five minutes before our mother would sign my sister up for the loony bin. Without Birdie and me around, she'd have a much, much easier time finding a new husband, which is #1 on *her* TO-DO LIST.

She made Birdie and me sit down last week on the living room sofa, and after she got comfortable in Daddy's brown chair with the hassock, she lit up an L&M that I bet she smokes instead of the Camels he did because they are her first initials—Louise Mary. She took a deep inhale and told us, "If we don't want to end up in the poor house, I need to find a new husband. I'm a catch, but nobody in his right mind wants to raise another man's children. I'll have to lure him in with my feminine wiles then break the bad news about you two once he falls for me." She blew a smoke ring that drifted over to Birdie's head and made her look like an angel with a halo. "So from now on, you two can't call me Mom or Mommy. Call me by my first name. At all times. Even at home, so you get into the habit. That way any eligible men we come across when we're shopping and such will think I'm your sister or aunt or a nice neighbor and they won't get scared off."

I was not shocked one iota by that idea. I can't forget for a second that our mother is not *just* beautiful, she's very, very smart. Not in a $64,000 Question way—she doesn't even know that the capital of North Dakota is Bismarck—but in a foxy way. I'd try to talk her out of this idea if it wasn't such a good one. We *do* need some money and getting a new husband would be very easy for her. She can wind men around her little finger. Daddy worshipped the ground she walked on. And when she takes us to the Lake Michigan beach in the summer, men fall over in the sand when they get a load of her toasty brown skin covered in baby oil when she's spread out on the white sheet 'cause she looks good enough to eat. And a lot of husbands up at church wink at her during Mass until their wives elbow them hard, and she can't walk down the street without a man in a car giving her a wolf whistle. If she could trap a rich husband with a good job, I bet her moods might even get better. So what if she wants us to pretend she's not our mother when she meets Mr. Tall, Dark, and Handsome at the movie theatre or the drug store until she can lure him into her spider web? Birdie and me will say, "See ya later, Louise," and just wander over to the candy aisle or out the door and all the way to *Oklahoma!* I love that movie!

But it'd be better if she could skip all that looking around for a new husband because that could take some time, and if they turn off the electricity because she can't pay the bill, that'd upset Birdie because she's so ascared of the dark. And for another thing, having to call her Louise all the time might not work out so hot either because my sister will have a really hard time remembering to do that since she drifts off and her memory is so terrible.

That's why I piped up and told our mother, "Gettin' a new husband is a swell idea, but if you wanna save on wear and tear, you could marry somebody you already know. Right away! Someone really nice!" My sister and me do NOT ever want another daddy, but I think the caretaker at the cemetery makes a pretty good living and he really likes Birdie and me. "You should get all dolled up tonight and go over to Holy Cross and visit Mr. McGinty after the sun sets."

Our mother threw her head back and cough-laughed for about an hour. "Joe McGinty? The man is a half-wit with a withered leg!" she said. "Are you outta your mind, Theresa?"

Back on the back porch on Daddy's pretend funeral day, since my sister is taking three turns in a row, I use that time to slide my ballpoint pen out of my shorts pocket and cross out #4: ~~Decide if I should go to the cops and confess to murdering Daddy~~ on my list and get back to working on #2: Convince Birdie that Daddy is really dead so Mom doesn't send her to the county insane asylum.

Forward.

"But," I say to my sister, who is now picking at a scab on her leg, "why would Daddy swim all the way to Boca Raton?" He was an excellent backstroker, but not that good. "Florida is really far away."

Like she's been practicing this in her spare time, Birdie says to me very smooth, "Because after he got the amnesia, he didn't remember anymore that he was supposed to come home and take care of us. Just like that man in *Mannix* who was in the car that went off the mountain and after he hit his head on the steering wheel he walked into the woods instead of going back to his family that was waiting for him to take them to church. Daddy just kept swimming and Boca Raton was just where he ended up, by accident."

That's really, really dumb, and I shouldn't "humor" her, but that's what they do to people in the movies so they don't jump off the ledge of a high building, which isn't very humorous, if you ask me. But what harm would it do to let her think, at least for a little while, that Daddy *is* living in Boca Raton with a bad case of amnesia? She's having such a tough time that if it makes her happy to believe that someday they will be together again, sooner rather than later, why not? I mean . . . hold the presses! That really *could* happen! Not the way that Birdie is thinking, but in another way. Look at Easter! I have not heard of another case of resurrection since you know whose, but that doesn't mean it isn't *possible*! Anything is. So once my sister gives up on believing that Daddy's still alive, we'll find his pretend grave, and then I'll talk her into that, "He's risen!" idea, and for a little while, I'll tell her that he's gonna come back like Jesus did and that will make her feel better too. I think. Like Doris Day says, "*Que sera, sera, whatever will be, will be, the future's not ours to see.*"

Anyways, there's no point in butting heads with Birdie over that resurrecting idea now. It took me over two months to convince her that it was the *Lone Ranger* not the *Long Ranger*, and that's just the tip of the iceberg. She thinks the name of the book with the fancy French man who was kept a prisoner in a tower, but then escaped, and came back to get revenge on the guys who treated him like dirt, is called *The Count of Monte Crisco*. I tried to explain to her that sounded more like a Julia Child cooking show and not a rip-roaring adventure story, but once she gets stuff in her head, it can get branded in there.

"Stop pickin' at yourself," I tell her. "You get blood on those socks, Mom, I mean, Louise, is gonna get mad." I take the Kleenex out of my pocket again and wipe off the stream that's trickling down her leg.

I can't decide what to tell her right this minute about Daddy being on the postcard in Dalinsky's, so thank the saints that she gives me a little more time to come up with something by having one of her driftings. It's because I told her that our mother would get mad at her.

While I'm thinking things over, a hearse pulls up in the cemetery.

I can't see one without the song named after them coming into my mind.

46

The worms crawl in, the worms crawl out,
the worms play pinochle in your snout.
They eat your eyes, they eat your nose,
they eat the jelly between your toes.

For a second, I feel so glad that Daddy is at the bottom of the lake and not worm food, but that feeling doesn't last long because I guess he's fish food, and considering how much he liked to catch them and fry them up in butter, if I was a trout, I'd be gunning for him too.

Trying to bring Birdie back from wherever it is she goes isn't always easy. Sometimes she sinks into a drifting like it's quicksand, but there are times I can run my finger down her arm and she'll go back to being as normal as she gets if I ask her, "S'awright?" in my Señor Wences voice. He's on the *Ed Sullivan Show*.

She doesn't answer back, "S'awright," because she can't do funny voices like I can. She's better at being the audience. She just smiles and picks another card out of the Candy Land deck like nothing happened. 'Cause she doesn't like orange, she scowls and sticks it on the bottom of the deck, and takes a blue card, which is fine by me. Who cares that she's a little cheat? What else does the poor kid have to live for?

After she moves four spaces, she says happily, "Someday Daddy'll get his memory back, just like that car-crash guy did and he'll come back to us. You'll see."

I look back at the hearse and say a quick Hail Mary even though I don't believe in God anymore, I still believe a little in his mother. I'm hoping that it's Daddy's pretend burial ceremony that's about to start on the other side of the fence, for Birdie's sake. If she could just see with her own eyes all the people saying goodbye to him, that would be so great.

For extra holy luck, I stroke our father's Swiss Army knife in my pocket that's next to my TO-DO LIST, and then I bring the St. Nicholas medal that Gammy gave me up to my lips and kiss it. I wear it around my neck because besides playing Santa Claus during Christmas, St. Nick is the patron saint of children and let's face it, Birdie and I need all the extra holy help we can get because whether you get to live or die . . . it's all about luck and we don't have that much.

Soldiers can go to dangerous places and come back without a scratch except for leaving a leg in Italy, or being shell-shocked like Audie Murphy, or Mr. McGinty, who had to have a dinner plate put into his head after he stepped on a land mind, but you make one wrong move like going fishing on a hot summer day with your kid who loves you so much that her heart feels like it might explode at any second from the missing, and it turns out to be the kiss of death. Any moron can see that every morning you get out of bed you're taking the chance that the Grim Reaper is waiting for you right around the corner.

I am saving up for some binoculars that I saw in the back of a *Superman* comic book—I got the idea from Mr. McGinty, who has a super-duper pair—but for now all I can do is squint my eyes to see if I can recognize any of the funeral faces on the other side of the black iron fence. Everyone is waiting for the casket to be slid out of the back of the black car by the Pauls, who have pink carnations pinned to their suit coats because that's one of the most popular funeral flowers there is. Gammy told me they stand for: I'll never forget you.

I don't see one person I know, which only goes to show you how hit and miss praying is. There's a hunched-over lady who is the saddest of the bunch. She's making a noise that sounds like a hurt dog. I want her to please, please, shut up because that sound is so awful and my heart is soaking it up like a sponge and I can't let that happen. One of the Finley sisters has to keep her head screwed on straight and it's too late for Birdie.

"Your turn," my sister and me say at the exact same time.

"Jinx!" I say quicker than her. "You owe me a dime!"

Birdie turns her smile upside down because another bad thing about her is that she can be a sore loser.

And a tightwad.

She's Got Enough Haunting Goin' On

Birdie doesn't take up much room in our bed after we say our special prayer and do our spooning because she sleeps in a balled-up fist. I was not born a good sleeper, but this is another thing my sister is excellent at when she isn't having nightmares or wetting the bed. Sun is coming through the cracks in our window shade, and I'm on my elbow studying her adorable face and feeling relieved that the sheet stayed dry last night because last week Louise hung one from the porch for the whole neighborhood to see. I am humming the special song louder and louder. I'm almost shouting it by the time she opens her eyes, that's how deep she sleeps.

I hook her straggly brown hair behind her ear and say, "Happy birthday, tweetheart. I got something for you." I reach into the crack between the bed and the wall. "Sorry it's not wrapped." Sticking a paper tube under your T-shirt and making it all the way out of the Five and Dime without the owner of the store noticing is almost impossible. Mrs. Kenfield has eyes in the back of her head.

When I hand over the gift, my sister makes her lips look like a tiny bird mouth—O. The nightlight will be a big help.

To show how much she likes her present, she gives me a butterfly kiss, my favorite. (Eskimo kisses are nice too, but can get snotty under certain conditions.) "Thank you, Tessie," she says with a lot of gratitude. "I got something for you too." She gets on her tummy and sticks her hand under the mattress on her side. "I know how much you wanted this."

It's the framed picture of Mom and Daddy that was on top of the bedroom vanity.

I grab it outta her hands and say, "Holy shit, Bird! Where'd you find it?"

She turns a lighter shade than pale and gives a little shiver. "In the black trunk in the attic. Alotta pictures of Daddy are in there."

"You went up to the attic?" I truly can't believe this for a couple of reasons. She is usually much too sweet to be sneaking around behind our mother's back, and a little heavy on her feet for a kid named Birdie. "Without me?"

I NEVER shoulda let her see *The Fly*. She doesn't understand that those horror movies are pretend. Even if I try to make fun of it by chasing her around the house saying, "*Help me . . . help me . . .*," in my excellent imitation of Vincent Price's voice after he became an insect, she screams bloody murder. So going up to attic? By herself? Where there are always alotta flies lying on the floor and windowsills? That only goes to show how much she adores me to death.

I reach over and give her a hug. "How about a joke to get our special day started off right!?"

She smiles and nods because that's what Daddy always did for us on our birthday.

"You got your thinking cap on?"

She pretends to place it on top of her head and tie it under her chin.

"Okay." I clear my throat that is always froggier sounding when I just wake up. "Where would you find a birthday present for a cat?"

Birdie thinks for a minute. "The pet store on 58th Street?"

"Nope."

"Ummm . . . I don't know. Where *would* you get a birthday present for a cat?"

I wait a beat the way Daddy taught me to before I deliver the punch line. "In the Sears and Roebuck catalog! Get it? CAT . . . alog?"

It takes her a second, but then she burst into giggles, and Mom must've heard her because she calls out of the kitchen, "Rise and shine, birthday ghouls!"

Calling us that lets us know that it's gonna be a good day, at least for awhile, because she's teasing us about our hobby instead of yelling about it. Part of her for-now happy mood is because she has always liked that Birdie and I were born on the same day one year apart—August 15th, the day of The Assumption. It's a Catholic holiday for the Virgin Mary. Our mother doesn't care so much about the Mother of Jesus heading up to Heaven, she's happy because she only has to bake one birthday cake. It's one of those killing-two-birds-with-one-stone situations since she not only hates cooking, believe me, she is no Betty Crocker. She would rather spend her precious time doing *her* hobbies.

HER ROYAL HIGHNESS'S FAVORITE THINGS

1. Looking at herself in the mirror or the toaster or the back of a skillet.
2. Paging through *Photoplay* magazines and saying impolite things about Ida Lupino.
3. Seeing Doris Day and Rock Hudson movies and then acting like she's Doris for the next week.
4. Going out to eat at a restaurant or supper club.
5. Being witchy to Birdie and me.

When my sister and me pad into the kitchen, our mother is already dressed and raring to go in a blue blouse and white pedal pushers. There are two packages lying next to a plate of jelly-filled donuts that she must've picked up from Meurer's Bakery because they're the best. I hope she saved the string off the white box for Birdie's cat's cradle game because she likes her strings fresh with the smell of sugar still on 'em.

One of the presents is small, the other is big. There are also two cards for each of us. One is in our mother's neat handwriting, and one is in our Gammy's not-so-neat handwriting. She has knobs growing on her fingers so it's hard to hold a pen.

Birdie and me tell Mom really loud, "Thank you!" and rip into both the donuts and Gammy's cards. Mine has a puppy on the front because I like them so much. Inside, she taped eleven dimes. Birdie's card has a rainbow on the front because even though she really likes puppies too, our grandmother can't send the same card to different kids, that's just not couth. Birdie only got ten dimes, of course.

On the bottom of both of our cards, she wrote the same thing:

xoxoxoxoxoxoxox
Wish your daddy was here.

Our mother says, "Goddamn her," and snubs out her cigarette on her plate. "This is exactly why I don't want you seeing her anymore. All she ever talks about is Eddie this and Eddie that. She couldn't let us have one day without reminding us?" And just like that, what had been looking like a sunny day goes gray, but then also, just like that, she smiles like something just dawned on her. "Open your presents!"

I say, "Age before beauty," and start to rip off the paper that has balloons on it. I was hoping for a tomahawk, but Mom got me a Nancy Drew book. I tell her, "Thank you! Thank you!" even though I have read the *The Haunted Showboat* already, it's a better present than what she gave me last year, which was a ventriloquist dummy. (Who in the hell is Charlie McCarthy?)

Birdie says, "My turn," and slowly takes the wrapping paper off her big present.

I get too excited to stand it, so I yell, "Hurry . . . hurry!" because I was the one who told Mom how much she wanted the dress and I can't wait to see her face. I don't like frilly things, but my sister is very, what Gammy calls, froufrou. Birdie saw this pink dress with at least ten petticoats in the window of Shuster's on North Avenue. The store sells regular shoes, but also ballet slippers, tap shoes, and dance costumes. She swooned down to the sidewalk and I had to prop her up all the way home, that's how much she loved the look of that fancy dress.

Birdie lifts up the box top with trembling fingers, separates the tissue paper, and right off by the look on her face I can tell that it's not what she'd been praying for night and day.

"Lemme see," I say.

Where the sparkles and a fluffy skirt should've been, there's a white Playtex girdle.

Somehow Birdie manages to say to our mother, "Thank you. I love it."

The saddest part of all of this is that Louise actually believes her. "Now nobody can call you Two-Ton Robin," she says, even though she's the only one who calls Birdie that. (In the tummy area, okay, my sister *is* a little tubby, but she doesn't weight 2,000 pounds, that's ridiculous.)

"Open your cards!" Mom says. "They're Hallmark!"

That's nice, because Birdie LOVES anything to do with Hallmark. Especially their Hall of Fame television shows. My card from Louise has a picture of a daisy on it which is also nice because she knows how much I like to garden with Gammy, and she can't stand Gammy any more than Gammy can stand her.

She signed both of our cards:

Love, Louise

There's a famous saying, "Actions speak louder than words," so I doubt that very much.

"I've got another surprise for you two," she says. "We're going on a birthday outing!"

"The zoo?" Birdie asks a little more chipper, because that's only about a mile from our house and she really loves Monkey Island and, of course, the bird house makes her conceited all day long.

Our mother says, "That's for me to know and for you to find out. Finish up your rolls and get dressed. And don't forget this, Robin Jean," she says as she lifts the Playtex girdle out of the box.

Birdie waits until we're back in our bedroom to ask, "Do I have to wear it?"

"Ummm . . . no." I think. "Tell her you tried it on and you really, really love it, but that it was too small. No, wait . . . tell her that it was way, way too big."

Birdie looks at her birthday present with welled-up eyes and says, "She won't believe me and then she'll get mad."

Since my sister *does* stink at lying, and our mother *will* get mad, I tell her, "Leave it up to me," and take the ugly girdle into the bathroom with me. I'm gonna splash water on my face and brush my teeth, and then I'll lie to Louise after I fish it out of the bowl. I'll tell her with my saddest face, "I was admiring it, thinking how thoughtful you are and what a great present it was, and I'm so, so sorry, but it slipped out of my fingers and fell into the toilet. Sorry."

Birdie and me are in the backseat of the woody wagon with all the windows open because it's always hot as hell on our birthday. Rock 'n roll music from WOKY is playing on the radio and our mother is singing along to a Bobby Daren song called *Dream Lover*. Maybe she's thinking about Daddy the same way I am. I used to like to sit back here and stare at the back of his neck where his hair hit his collar, it was cute and jagged.

My sister has her head stuck all the way out the car window because she likes the way rushing air feels on her face no matter how many times I tell her she's gonna get her head chopped off by a passing car. This is the famous saying, "throwing caution to the wind." For such a jumpy kid, she does this kind of thing too much for my liking. When she gets in a certain kind of mood, she can get, oh, I don't know . . . a wild streak? This summer, she rang Mr. Johnson's doorbell and ran away one night when we were doing some spying. Nobody knows him that good because he doesn't go to our church, but every kid in the neighborhood does know that he will chase after you if you bother him. I was sweating bullets, but I could tell by the look on Birdie's face when we were peeling down the block that she didn't care if Mr. Johnson caught her and took her down into his basement and made her head look like the deer he has hanging in his living room because Lutherans like to stuff things for fun instead of playing bingo.

I tug on my sister's leg and tell her to put her head back in the car one more time and when she doesn't listen to me one more time, I give up and ask our mother, "Where are we?" I don't know this part of Milwaukee.

"This is the South Side. Where all the Polacks live," Mom says with a snort because even the *least* funniest person I know has to agree that Polacks are the people with the best jokes.

I take a Kleenex out of my pocket and wipe sweaty Birdie down, and then I stare out the window and hope that wherever our mother is taking us is not dumb like the time she took us swimming in the middle of winter to a place called a natatorium. Birdie couldn't stand the way the place smelled, and I can't even do the dead man's float.

When we finally get off the expressway and make a couple of turns, she says, "Look!" and points to a sign over our heads:

WELCOME TO THE 1959 WISCONSIN STATE FAIR

Birdie and me have never heard of something like this, so we don't know what to expect. We just say, "Thank you!" because you have to for even the littlest thing.

After she parks the car, Mom says, "C'mon. This way!" She's almost skipping. She can get like this, not often, but she can. Real perky. "I loved the Fair when I was a kid and you're gonna love it too!"

There are alotta people of all shapes and sizes and ages. Looking at them is very interesting. Mother takes us to a sideshow where there is a *Woman of a Thousand Veils* and a baby in a bottle and an enormously fat lady and a sword swallower. And there are rides galore. A huge roller coaster, merry-go-rounds, a Ferris wheel, and people are selling food. There's also a man who will guess your weight if you give him a quarter. Birdie started breathing fast when we walked past him, so I said really quick to our mother, "Gosh, I'm hot and starving. I think I'm gonna faint." (This is one of the stunts I pull if things aren't going very well. Kids go woozy in church all the time because they gotta fast before they take Holy Communion, so fainting is something that really does happen.) I cannot let Louise get it into her head that it'd be a great idea to get my sister up on that gigantic scale. She loves to be right, and the bigger the audience, the better. She's always making cracks about "Two-ton Robin," outside the church after Mass on Sunday.

After Louise buys us hot dogs with pickle relish and mugs of Graf's frosty root beer that are so good that Bird cries a little, she checks her watch and says, "You've got time to do one more thing while I run and get us a box of cream puffs. How about you go look at the farm animals?"

"That's a great idea, but no, thank you," I say, because I'm pretty sure she's trying to make us get hoof-and-mouth disease. "If you don't mind . . . we wanna go to the Spook House, right, Bird?" We have passed it a few times and it looked dark and cool and the both of us are sweating up a storm, especially my sister, whose hand feels like a raw chicken drumstick in mine. And getting scared . . . that reminds me of Daddy. A good *Gotcha!* would almost make me feel like he was here with us.

After we weave around the crowds to the ticket booth in front of the Spook House, Louise heads over to a building marked Home Economics, and Birdie and I head through the KEEP OUT! HAUNTED! doors in a red, rumbling cart. Creepy stuff jumps out at us. Skeletons and grisly looking zombies and ghosts and cobwebs brush against our skin. I love it, even though it's kinda cheesy because you can see the strings on the bats, but Birdie hates it. She wet her pants because she took all of it too much to heart, and because she crawled into my lap, the pee is all over me too. I shoulda known that she's got enough haunting going on. I tried to mop us off, but that was a loosing battle because she'd just had that root beer.

We are waiting in front of the ride for Louise, who is coming toward us with a bakery box. When she gets to us, she notices our wet shorts right off. She points down and says, "What happened?"

I tell her, "Oh, they had a witch in there and . . . and she threw water on us . . . *hardy hardy har*," but I figured out too late that our blouses would also be soaked because Louise kinda sprung that on me, so that's another thing I better put on my next TO-DO LIST: Think faster.

On the ride home, our mother lets us know how mad she is at us by eating one of the cream puffs and making a big deal over how tasty it is every two seconds—"Oh, yum . . . yum," and not giving us any. Birdie is drooling from wanting to have that deliciousness in her mouth and I've run out of Kleenexes, so I have to wipe off her mouth with the bottom of my T-shirt.

I spent the trip looking out the car window wondering if Louise'd be sorry for being so cruddy to us after my sister and me save up enough money selling potholders to our neighbors to run away to _____? I'm not sure yet where Birdie and I will go, maybe to Gammy and Boppa's, or to Oklahoma, where all the mornings are beautiful, but I also wouldn't mind following James Darren's suggestion: "*Goodbye cruel world, I'm off to join the circus.*" Or maybe we could be part of the Freak Show we saw today. We could let the fat lady with the three chins be our mother. She told us that she couldn't have kids when we were staring at her behind the sideshow glass, and then she burst into tears. Probably because she was hungry. She would get along great with my sister.

When the Moon Hits Your Eye

When our mother gets mad, it's not like a sudden storm that blows in and out. Hers is more like what the weatherman with the cute black cat named Albert on the TV's Channel Four calls, "A stalled front."

The second we got home, she sent us straight to the basement to wash out our pee shorts. We could hear her in the kitchen pacing above our heads.

Birdie, who is huddled over next to the furnace, says, "I'm sorry. I couldn't help it. That ride was so scary and now . . . now Mom's gonna punish both of us."

"You mean *Louise* is gonna punish both of us," I say as I shove the pink shorts in the washer. "You gotta remember to call her that, okay?"

I shake in some Tide powder, and then turn on the washer the same way I do with the sheet that she wets in the middle of the night. Only then, I have to climb on top of the Maytag and sit up there and read a *Superman* comic book with our flashlight until the spinning cycle is done because the washer doesn't sit right on the floor and it makes this horrible banging noise that would wake Louise up.

"C'mere." I hold out my hand to Birdie and lead her

back across the cement floor that hasn't been swept in ages. There's a dead mouse in one of the traps because it was Daddy's job to throw them away, and spider webs on the walls, and the worst of all—flies on the sills that could be dead or just playing possum. I sit my sister down on the bottom basement step, put my arm around her, and say, "You wanna hear a happy story?"

She nods, because she really does need cheering up. She wanted one of those cream puffs so bad.

I say, "Remember our last birthday? How we all went to Mama Mia's restaurant and we had that delicious sausage pizza and fat, spongy bread drenched in butter . . . and how Mom and Daddy ate a plate of spaghetti with meatballs and drank wine like Lady and the Tramp to celebrate ten years of being married, and how that nice waitress with the black teased-up hair cleared our dishes and then came back and dropped a little something else off at the table along with the check?" I make my voice sound like hers. "'Here's your doggie bagga. Thank youa verya mucha,'" and I told her, "But we can't take that under false pretenses because that's against the law and a sin. My sister and me want one really bad, but we don't have a dog."

And then Daddy, and even Mom laughed real hard, and . . . and on the way home he sang to her, '*When the moon hits your eye like a big-a pizza pie, that's amore,*' and she loved it so much that she didn't care what a mess that would make of her face and she even set her head on his shoulder and let her hair get messy."

Birdie smiles, but it's a ghost of a one that I can see through. She looks like she might bawl some more. I try not to, because our mother calls us babies, and sometimes will sing, "*Cry me a river*," but we're down here alone, so I might let out a few of the tears that I can feel brimming over. I'm sad because it feels good to remember the fun times we had with Daddy, but it's a bad thing too because having the memories make me wish we could make more of them and now we'll never, ever get to. Everything Birdie and me ever loved doing with him we'll never get to do again. No more fishing, no more laughing at his jokes, no more bedtime hugs, no more singing the *Sisters* song at Lonnigan's, no more *Gotchas!*

And it's not only thinking about what *already* happened, it's also thinking about any dreams that Birdie and me had for the future. Like someday getting a pooch of our own, or going to the Wisconsin Dells to see the giant Paul Bunyan statue with Daddy when he saved up enough tips. That will never happen because beetle-browed Stan was right about what he said the night after he and Jim rescued me outta the white motorboat. "Her life ain't ever gonna be the same." Birdie's neither.

I have been trying to believe in that famous saying, "Time heals all wounds." My sister and me hear people saying that at the cemetery all the time, but I've reached the conclusion that's just something people tell people when they fall apart in front of their eyes instead of telling them, "Sorry that pain you're feeling will never, ever, ever, ever, ever, ever, ever go away." I don't want to believe that, but I think that's the truth. Maybe many, many years from now a scab will form on Birdie's broken heart because she didn't murder Daddy, but I think mine will be taking a licking until the end of time.

"What's taking you so long?" Louise yells at us from the back hallway. "Get up here."

I tell Birdie who's gone stiff as a stiff, "Let's spiff you up, kiddo," and then I swipe her blah-brown bangs away from her eyes and lick my finger to straighten her eyebrows. I check under her nails for dirt too; Louise hates that. "You look beautiful and very skinny. Time to face the music."

Birdie is still so rigid that I have to carry-lug her up the basement steps, that's how ascared she is of our mother's stupid punishments.

Louise is tapping her foot and inspecting her fingernail polish at the kitchen table. That's where she spends most of her time when she isn't staring at herself, or bothering Birdie and me. She changed out of the blouse and pedal pushers she wore to the Wisconsin State Fair. Now a pretty white top and a full yellow skirt and white high heels that she only gets to wear during the summer are making her look good. Her wavy red hair is piled high on her head in a French twist. She's freshened up her makeup too. Instead of her usual red lipstick, she's got on a really pink shade that I've never seen before.

To smooth down her ruffled feathers, it's always good to start out with a compliment. "We love your new shade of lipstick, don't we, Robin Jean?" Louise can't see my sister nod her head because she's hiding behind me, but I can feel it brushing against my back.

"I'm going out," Louise says. "The cream puffs are in the fridge."

Holy cow! What a big surprise! How come she didn't mention Birdie's peeing in her pants in the spook house a hundred more times? Why isn't she punishing us? How come she's letting us have that nice dessert? This is VERY suspicious. Maybe because it's our birthday? And down there, somewhere, she must have a heart that got thawed a little in all this heat?

Before Louise can change her mind, Birdie and me both rush to tell her, "Thank you . . . thank you!"

But my sister also says, "You're so pretty. Where are you going? Can we come with you?"

I don't have to ask Louise where she's going. She'll tell us that she's heading to confession, but she isn't. Any idiot knows that they don't have nighttime confession, and second off, she's religious, but not *that* religious. I knew she wasn't telling us the truth the first night she took off and left Birdie and me alone because she does this funny thing with her mouth when she's lying. Twists it to the left a little. I was so curious that I wanted to put on black clothes and follow her to see what she was really up to because that's what they do on TV, but Birdie was too ascared.

I found out where Louise really went by searching her jacket pockets when she drove over to the Red Owl the next day. It kinda made me laugh when I found the balled up Lonnigan's cocktail napkin in her pocket because she only lied to us a little. Daddy sometimes called the bar, "The Confessional," because after people get drunk they'll cry in their beers and tell you all sorts of bad things they've done and how sorry they are. There was a name and telephone number scribbled in blue pen on the napkin.

Dwight Anderson   Hilltop 4-5271

I figured he must be a friend of our father's; he had so many. To know Eddie Finley was to love Eddie Finley! Everyone did, not just Birdie and me. Louise won't talk about him anymore, and I was feeling so desperate to hear a good story about him that maybe I hadn't heard before that I called the number on the napkin. But when a man picked up and said, "Anderson residence. Dwight speaking," I chickened out and said, "*Vaya con Dios,*" in my Zorro voice and hung up.

After Louise pushes back her kitchen chair and heads toward the front door, I tug my hand out of my sister's, tell her, "Stay here. Be right back. Eat one of those cream puffs," and I go after our mother.

She is yanking her raincoat out of the front hall closet. The metal hanger falls onto the wooden floor and she doesn't pick it up. "Please don't be mad at Birdie for having an accident in her shorts," I tell her. "Daddy wouldn't be."

She places her hand on the front door latch. Around the fourth finger on her tan left hand there's a ghost wedding ring where the real one used to be. She doesn't look at me, just says, "Your father's not here anymore."

I reach out and place my hand on top of hers. Her skin is so soft. "Mom?"

She scowls.

"Sorry. Louise?" I take my hand away. "Can Birdie and me come with you to Lonnigan's tonight?"

It'd be really nice to see the old gang, to breathe in the smell of Pabst Blue Ribbon and peanuts, and to see them raise their glasses in a toast to, "The best bartender in the parish!"

Louise shoves the screen door open and says, "Clean up the house and take baths," and walks out into the drizzling night. A few minutes later, she fires up the woody station wagon that everyone on the block can hear. Daddy had been meaning to replace that muffler for the longest time.

Sometimes You Gotta Take Your Life into Your Hands

After I put a bag of dog poop on Mrs. Klement's front porch, light it on fire, and run away to get back at her for reporting to Louise that she saw me stealing my sister's birthday nightlight, Birdie and me get down to work. We pretend the whole time that we're two of those elves that surprise the shoemaker by tidying up his workshop while he's sleeping. She loves that game, especially when I do my elf voice that really sounds more like one of Snow White's dwarves—Grumpy—because cleaning is a big waste of time when I could be working on more important things like spying and blackmailing, or my TO-DO LIST.

Once everything is shipshape, I grab both of Birdie's hands, squeeze hard, and say, "Okay. Stop. Bath time." If I don't get bossy she won't stop polishing because she really, really loves shiny things. She inherited that from Louise.

We shampoo each other in the tub with the scary claw feet that I wrap towels around so Birdie doesn't have to look at them. When we duck under the water to rinse our heads, we practice our mermaid talking. This could also be a good carnival job because they had a lady up on the stage who had scales all over her at the State Fair, so maybe we could team up with her in a partnership like Bob Hope and Bing Crosby or Dean Martin and Jerry Lewis. Instead of me singing and dancing and doing voices and Birdie beating everyone in cat's cradle and performing card tricks, we could be The Electrifying Finley Mermaids and dive into the tank with Elsie the Fish Woman. That has a nice ring to it. Of course, I'd have to learn how to swim first, but maybe Mr. McGinty could teach me in the cemetery pond the way he told me he would.

"Birdie Finley," I say underwater.

She bubbles back, "Tessie Finley," but when she does it tonight instead of making me smile, a picture of Daddy sinking to the bottom of the lake comes into my mind and I get out of the tub real fast so she does too.

My sister smells much better after the bath. Like Ivory soap and Breck shampoo and not like the cafeteria up at school on mock chicken leg day. We're in our bed, lying on top of our sheet. She's on her tummy and I'm making rows on her back and pretending to plant lavender because Gammy, who is such an excellent gardener, told me it can help a person sleep. I didn't before, but I know now why they're called the "wee" hours, so I'm gonna ask Gammy the next time I see her what flower keeps a person from peeing in the bed and I'll start planting those on Birdie's back every night. It'll probably be one of the yellow ones, maybe daisies.

After I've sowed the lavender, we get under the sheet, say our prayer, and make a tent with our feet and lift it up and down because it gives us a nice breeze.

Birdie starts crying, "Daddy, Daddy, Daddy, please come back from Boca Raton."

I tell her for the hundredth millionth time, "He's not in Boca Raton, tweetheart. He's dead."

I almost have a heart attack when she sobs back, "I know! Yesterday when I told Mr. Dalinsky that it was our Daddy on the postcard, he laughed, and told me that . . . that the man looks a lot like Daddy, but it's not. He's just a man called a model that they paid to look happy next to a big fish so people will come to Florida to catch one too."

Even though I owe Mr. Dalinsky for telling her what I've been telling her all along is true, I wouldn't mind setting his stupid store on fire for laughing at my sister. I would get gasoline in a paper cup from the Clark station. But when you are doing a crime, you can't have any witnesses who could rat you out to the cops, so I'd have to do that on one of the days "The Peeker" isn't working at the station because he never takes his eyes offa me when I go up there. He's told me three times that he loves redheads. "Ya know, like Lucille *Ball*," and then he laughed. I think it was a laugh, whatever it was, I never wanna hear it again.

I pat Birdie to calm her down, stroke her hair, and after she curls up against me, I take the folded up paper and pencil out from under my pillow and add Mr. Dalinsky to:

MY SHIT LIST

1. ~~Dennis Patrick.~~
2. The greasy man who tries to peek in the gas station bathroom window when you can't make it home

from the Tosa Theatre after you drink a large root beer.
3. Mrs. Gertrude Klement.
4. ~~Mom.~~ Louise.
5. Jenny Radtke.
6. Mr. Dalinsky.

I'm worried that when the owner of the drug store told Birdie that Daddy was really dead that she started wailing. I can only hope she didn't do that really loud and in front of one of the gossipy ladies from the Pagan Baby Society because they would talk about her at their next Monday night meeting, and then Louise will know for sure that Birdie has gone around the bend.

That was so stupid of me to send her up there in the first place. Selfish. I needed her out of the way, and knowing that she can't resist a brown cow, or me, I lied and told her that I wasn't feeling good and gave her a dollar from my piggy bank so she could get herself a float and me some Tums, even though I knew that wasn't the ginchiest idea because she'd probably just stand in that air-conditioned store and stare at that stupid picture postcard taped up to the cash register for an hour. It was a gamble, and I lost. But who knows? Maybe it'll turn out okay in the long run because at least she knows now that Daddy really *is* at the bottom of Lake Michigan and not catching pointy-nosed fishes in Boca Raton.

Once Birdie skipped far enough down the block yesterday that I was sure she wasn't going to double back, I checked to make sure that Mrs. Klement was at confession and couldn't spy on me some more from her stool in the back window, and I hopped over the cemetery fence to do another one of what the cavalry calls scouting missions. Birdie hasn't been coming with me to look for Daddy's pretend grave because she didn't want to face the truth, but I've been sneaking away when she was busy cleaning or doing something else for Mother, like giving her a foot rub, so when the day came that she finally *did* believe that he really *is* dead—like she does now—I could take her straight to him.

I looked and looked until I bumped into Mr. McGinty not far from the pond where Daddy and me used to fish. That was odd, because Mr. McGinty usually only digs graves, mows, and pulls weeds right after the sun comes up or close to when it's about to set, so there is less chance that he'll run into visitors because he is very shy except around Birdie and me. He doesn't get out of the cemetery much, only to early Mass, and he buys food, but I have never seen him at the grocery store. Secretly, I think that he takes care of more than just the cemetery. I think he keeps his eye out for, and on, the Finley sisters. Did Daddy ask him to do that in case anything happened to him because our mother is 100% Irish and it's a well-known fact that they are not good with kids? That seems possible because Daddy really liked Mr. McGinty. "Pipe down, Louise. Joe's a little cracked, but he's still a good egg," he used to tell her when she would complain about Birdie and me going over to Holy Cross to visit with him.

Even though I gave him the signal to let him know that I was nearby the way Mr. McGinty told me I had to because he's not good with *Gotchas!*, when I said, "Hi," he jumped about a foot in the air, dropped his shovel on his foot, and yelped something that I couldn't make out. That's another reason why he'd be a great daddy because he'd understand Birdie's jitteriness. "Sorry," I said. "I whistled really loud."

He took a clean, white hankie out of his pocket, mopped the sweat off his forehead, and said, "Good afternoon, Tess." He has the nicest voice. It reminds me of Mr. Ed Herlihy's. He does the Kraft commercials on the television. Those are Birdie's favorite ads because she really loves cheese.

He's tall, so I usually have to crank my head back when I talk to him, but yesterday he was standing in the grave, so we were almost face-to-face. He gets a lot of weather on his 'cause people die all the time and they gotta get buried during the summer, fall, winter, and spring, so his skin looks pretty used. His nose runs on the large side, not like Jimmy Durante's or anything, but biggish, his cheekbones jut out like cliffs, and his hands have a lot of calluses. His blond hair sprouts up on his head like new grass, shorter even than a crew cut, so you can see his scalp. (Apaches would love him.) All in all, he's a fine-looking gentleman. And his leg isn't withered the way Louise said it was when I told her that she should come over here to talk to him about getting married. It's just got alotta red and pink scars and is tender to the touch.

I didn't know how bad I missed him until I saw him. I toed some of the dirt that he'd piled up next to the grave and said, "I feel crummy about not coming to see ya since. . . ." We have things in common. We both like being around dead people, and he can't sleep either. He hasn't come by for awhile, but out of habit, I still keep a look out for him from our bedroom window. On certain summer nights, he waves a lantern on the other side of the cemetery fence. We go frog hunting and firefly catching. He also taught me some of the constellations, but other than pointing out the Big and Little Dippers and such, we don't talk a lot because Mr. McGinty is the strong, silent type. "I don't know if you heard . . . our daddy died."

"I know that, honey. I dug—" In his brown eyes with the lids that are always dropped to half-mast, I could see that he felt bad. Even if Louise doesn't think of him as husband material, I almost asked him to be our new daddy right then and there. Maybe he could grow on our mother over time. I didn't like Charlie Garfield the first day I met him and now look at us. We're practically going steady. Mr. McGinty says, "I been watching you comin' over the fence." With his war binoculars, I bet. He uses them to watch out for, "Intruders." He can see right into Birdie's and my bedroom, that's how powerful they are. "How come your sister hasn't been with you? She okay?"

I don't want to lie to him because I like him so much, but I also don't want to go into a long explanation about how weird she's going, so I just say, "Birdie's been resting up. She'll be coming over any day now."

He cracks his knuckles, which is a bad habit of his, and says, "I don't worry about you so much, you're strong in the legs, but your sister. . . ." He has warned me about this many, many times. She has always made it over the fence okay, but there is a first time for everything. She has that chubby tummy that she might forget to suck in all the way and it could get caught up on the points. "Wouldn't want her to get hurt."

Mr. McGinty frets all the time about bad things happening. I would too, if I were him. He's told me some war stories. How any of those GI Joes come back after the war and be normal after they got chased around by the Nazi people, bayoneted left and right, and saw bombs blow up their friends is a mystery to me. How can they go back to being a regular fella that works at the Feelin' Good Cookie factory or American Motors with all those bad memories running around in the brains? That's where most of the dads around here have their jobs. They can also be tool and die makers, like Charlie's father is. I pointed at Mr. McGinty's grave-digging shovel one afternoon and told him, "You're a tool and die maker too," but he didn't think that was funny. This is something we *don't* have in common. He doesn't joke or watch detective shows or go to the movies or sing, none of that. He doesn't go in for exciting mystery stories either. He reads religious books and says the rosary on his day off. All his pants have knee patches from praying so much.

I tell him, "Thank you for worrying about Birdie climbing the fence, but sometimes you don't have any choice. Sometimes you gotta take your life into your hands no matter how scary something is, right?" I thought saying that would make him feel a little better about being a war hero even if he's got a dinner plate in his head and a screwed-up leg, but he didn't take that well. He hopped up out of the grave really fast and took off. He didn't even stop when I yelled after him, "Hey! You forgot your shovel!"

When I was watching him hip-hop away, I realized again how stupid, stupid, stupid I've been. Instead of searching for Daddy's pretend grave every chance I get, I shoulda just asked Mr. McGinty where it was before he hightailed it back to his shack, which is a lot bigger in the inside than it looks from the outside.

He keeps the place very clean. There's a small table that has a checker board set up on it because we play sometimes. And instead of paintings in frames, he has holy cards stuck to the wall above his sofa that turns into a bed. He collects religious cards, the same way some of the boys in the neighborhood collect steely marbles. His favorite is the one of the patron saint of the dead—St. Gertrude—which I think is kinda funny because that's my most mortal enemy, Mrs. Klement's, first name. (She thinks she's a saint, but she's NOT holier than thou.) I had to trade four St. Jude's for the St. Gert card because it's very rare, but Mr. McGinty loved it so much that he gave me his purple heart because he knows it's my favorite color.

He's also very keen on St. Joan of Arc because she was a soldier who fought for what she believed in too, which wasn't Uncle Sam, but God. We had a talk about this under the stars one night. I agreed with him that she was brave, yes, "But she was stupid too, because she didn't really think her plan all the way through." Things were going okay for Joan for awhile, but in the end, some French people burned her up like a steak. God the all-powerful coulda saved her, the same way he coulda saved Daddy, so that only goes to show you that: 1. You have to be very, very careful about who you stick up for in life. I wouldn't fight a battle for anybody but Birdie, and Gammy, if Boppa wasn't around. 2. What the nuns and priests teach you about the Almighty loving you and taking care of you? That's nothing but hot air a.k.a. bullshit.

Even though Birdie has stopped whimpering, I keep stroking her back in our bedroom that's not as dark as it used to be because of the birthday nightlight. Her skin isn't satiny smooth like it is in the winter, it's more like fly paper. "I'm so sorry that Daddy isn't in Boca Raton like you thought he was. I really, really am." I tell her more nice things like that so they really sink in. "But now that you've faced the music, we gotta do what the state motto says. We gotta move forward. How 'bout we head over to the cemetery tomorrow? We can bring a picnic when Louise goes to try for that job at Turner's Toppers. After we eat, we'll look around for Daddy, or we could just ask Mr. McGinty where the pretend grave is." Birdie doesn't hop up and down over that idea because finding out that the model in the postcard isn't Daddy really took the wind outta her sails. She's kinda limp. "You'll feel a lot better after we find him." I'm so sure that this would be the best present I could ever give her. "I promise."

She doesn't say anything back, so I think she mighta fallen asleep. It's a miracle how she can drop off to Dreamland and doesn't wake up at all during the night. You could set off a cherry bomb in our bedroom and she wouldn't move a muscle in one of her arms that she keeps crossed over her chest like she's in a casket, which scares me so bad some nights that I pinch her to make sure she didn't die, and even that doesn't wake her up, she just groans a little.

I lean over Birdie and push down the alarm button that

I set for 5 a.m. in case she wets the bed, which I'm pretty positive that she's gonna do because she always pees during the nights that things don't go so hot with our mother during the day. After what happened at the fair, I'm expecting a flood. On top of that, raindrops are beating against our window.

I lie flat and make a coupla sheet angels, not big ones, because our bed isn't that large. I'm just about to start practicing "My Favorite Things" for when I enter the Miss America contest, when Birdie says, "But . . . even if we find his grave, Daddy's not really in there. You told me that he's at the bottom of—"

"Part of him *is* in the coffin. His soul, and that's much more important than his bones and a bunch of rotting flesh."

If she was a little smarter, she could figure out that's a lie because Daddy's soul isn't in the pretend grave, it's in Heaven with all the other good peoples' who don't lie or want to set fire to drugstores or let their fathers drown.

"But what if Louise comes home from trying for that job at the hat shop and she . . . she catches us?" Birdie whispers. "She'd be so mad. I don't want a spanking."

Our mother never liked it when we visited the cemetery to practice our hobby when Daddy was still alive, but after he drowned, and Mrs. Klement told her that she saw me goin' over there out her kitchen window, Louise blew her top. She tells us at least once a day now, "If I *ever* catch you climbing into that graveyard again, or hear from anybody else that you did"—she means Gert, who has nothing better to do with her measly life than spend it keeping track of my every move—"mark my words, the

Finley ghouls won't be able to sit down for a week."

Louise *could* make my life easier by taking us to Daddy's pretend grave if she wanted to, but she doesn't visit it, and she doesn't want Birdie and me to either because she's trying to act like he never even existed. She told us, "Life goes on." She never talks about him, and she hid all his pictures in the attic trunk and gave his things away, even his fishing pole that I wanted to keep so bad that I got down on my knees in front of her and said, "Please?" I stupidly thought she was going to be nice for a minute, but then she set her chin and said, "If he hadn't gone fishing that day, he'd still . . . ," and rushed out of the living room with the pole in her hand.

I get up on my elbow to tell Birdie a little white lie. "I looked it up in the *Encyclopaedia Britannica* at the library. Applying for a job at a hat shop takes four hours and we won't stay over at the cemetery nearly that long." I use my Señor Wences voice because she loves it. "S'awright?"

I think she mighta drifted off because she doesn't laugh like she usually would, but then she says in her sleepy voice, "Thank you again for my nightlight. It's really nice. You love your present as much as I love mine?"

"Even more, I bet. That was so brave of you to go up to the attic." I got the picture of Daddy wedged down deep against the wall on my side of the bed so Louise won't find it. I pick Birdie's hand up in mine. "Let us pray." We don't bow our heads and recite the now I lay me down to sleep prayer that they taught us a school. Birdie and me always say, "I love you two as much as the stars and the moon," because that's what Daddy used to tell us after he tucked us in for the night.

After Birdie falls asleep for real, I don't feel like singing anymore, so I'm making hand shadows on the wall and thinking how a lot of people around here want to be more "modern" and "with it." They want cars with big fins and automatic dishwashers and diamond jewelry, but listening to the rain pitter-pattering against our bedroom window, and feeling my sister's sticky body next to mine, and every so often reaching down and stroking the picture of our Daddy and pressing his Swiss Army knife against my cheek makes me feel sure that the old days are good enough for me and the Bird.

Most Things in Life Sound Better Than They Are Except for Blackmail

We didn't find Mr. McGinty, or Daddy's grave, the first time we tried, or the second day either, but today is gonna be different. Those other visits to the cemetery had to be quick ones because Birdie was still getting used to the idea of going behind Louise's back—she was jumpier than a Mexican bean—but like I tell her when I'm cooking up our breakfast on the green stove this morning, "You know that famous saying . . . third time's the charm?"

It's gotta be.

I need to check the last thing off my list or throw in the towel. I don't want to, Daddy would be so disappointed in me, but tomorrow is the first day of sixth grade. I'll be so busy diagramming sentences and learning dumb historical facts and getting my ears pinched by those mean nuns who keep us prisoners until 3:30. And then after school, I'll have to do my homework and Birdie's too, and tell Louise thank you and how gorgeous she is every two minutes that I won't have time to sneak over to the cemetery. Even worse, I had to add something extra onto #3 last night, so that's gonna make it even harder.

TO-DO LIST

1. ~~Talk Mom into letting Birdie and me go to Daddy's pretend funeral.~~
2. ~~Convince Birdie that Daddy is really dead so Mom doesn't send her to the county insane asylum.~~
3. If #1 and #2 don't work out, find Daddy's pretend grave in the cemetery when Mom isn't around so Birdie can say goodbye to him once and for all because seeing really is believing. P.S. The resurrecting idea you had is a good one. Don't forget to tell her that.
4. ~~Decide if I should confess to the cops about murdering Daddy.~~

Louise is almost done getting ready for work because she got the job at the hat shop. She still does the grocery shopping because she could bump into a man in the Red Owl's meet department (joke!), but since she needs her, "Beauty rest," I'm in charge now of getting food on the table in the morning and at supper. I only know how to make a coupla things. Scrambled eggs, fried Spam, and one of my daddy's favorites, sloppy joes. That's what I made last night because we had hamburger in the fridge and tomato paste in the pantry. We didn't have any buns, so I scooped the slop onto pieces of stale Wonder bread, which gave it a nice crunch. (Sloppy joes still make me get choked up, so I slipped mine to Birdie under the table.)

The eggs are nice and fluffy this morning. I think I'm getting pretty great at cooking. Maybe I'll be a detective who also owns a coffee shop someday and Birdie could be a waitress that everyone would come to order breakfast from because she's so damn cute.

"You look just like Doris Day. How did it go yesterday?" I ask Louise when she comes out of the bedroom in a peach dress and white heels. When she sits down at the table, I slide the eggs outta the pan onto a plate and set it down in front of her. "Did you sell many hats?"

She won't answer me, but I have to keep trying to break the ice. She's not mad at us, for once. She's ticked-off because Daddy died, so now she has to work for a living. Birdie and me are two days into one of her cold shoulders that started after the fourth day she took the bus to—TURNER'S TOPPERS—to start the salesgirl job because we were down to our last dime. Louise was excited about getting dressed up and out of the house, at first, but that wore off by the third day when her feet started to hurt, and she began hating waiting on people like she's, "Some kind of servant."

I spoon up a bite of eggs and try again. "Do you like working with Mrs. Turner?" People say there are no dumb questions, but that one is. Just having to listen to the shop owner's nasally voice all day would upset anybody's tummy. Even God can't stand it. I heard that Father Ted had to fire her from the choir a few months ago because her mucus singing was making the congregation throw up their Holy Communion wafers. "Does her husband ever tell her a good story about Boppa that she tells you when you're sorting out the hats?" Mr. Turner is a teller at the same First Wisconsin Bank that my grandfather works at.

Boppa used to be a fireman, but he keeps money safe now from bank robbers. He's a guard with a gun, but he also plays practical jokes on the customers too. He spends every Saturday morning at Ernie's Magic Shop on Center Street buying hand buzzers, gum that turns your teeth black, and snakes that jump outta peanut cans. "Has she heard about any great tricks he pulled lately?"

This is the longest Birdie and me have gone without seeing our grandparents since we've been born and we miss them so bad. Daddy used to take us out to their stone house in the country every Sunday, but Louise won't let us visit them. I think she's still steamed that they couldn't give her more cash than twenty dollars at the funeral. They can't help it if they don't have a pot to pee in.

Birdie said to me last week, "I miss Gammy and Boppa. Can you call them up and tell them to come over here?"

I did like she asked, but maybe they couldn't hear the phone ringing because they were crying doubly loud since Daddy is the second kid they've lost. Their daughter died before I was born so I have only seen pictures of her in an old scrapbook. She was an itty-bitty thing, like Birdie, but her name was Alice. I don't know which sickness Alice had because Gammy keeps mum on the subject. She lets her flowers do the talking. She planted a memory garden at her house for her dead daughter, and I bet she does the same for her dead son when spring comes again. I'll help her, so that will prove that famous saying, "a labor of love," is true because she won't pay me, but that's okay. I have some other ideas how to get money in case Louise quits her job because she can't stand waiting on people or hearing Mrs. Turner's nasally voice, or if she doesn't find a husband. If we can't pay the rent, sleeping under the stars instead of a roof might not be that bad, but we still need to eat, especially Birdie.

I won't deliver the *Sentinel* newspaper on our red Schwinn the way some of the boys in the neighborhood do. Just like I do every Friday to check what's playing at the Tosa Theatre, I'll ride our bike over to Bloomers on Fond du Lac Avenue and ask the owner, Mr. Yerkovich, if I could make vases up for him because I know a lot about flowers from playing in the cemetery, but also from working in the garden with Gammy. Alotta people die and get married around here, so Mr. Y has to work hard on so many funeral arrangements and wedding bouquets that his wrists got sprained and now they're permanently floppy, so he could probably use the help. I might even be able to teach him a thing or two since I am half-English and flowers are in my blood same as they are in Gammy's. They are not in Boppa's. Mischief runs in his veins because his family came from the same Old Country that our mother's family came from—the Emerald Island—which *sounds* really luxurious, but I think, like a lot of things in life, it sounds a lot better than it really is. Except for that pot of gold at the end of the rainbow . . . I could really go for that! If I could find Louise some treasure, she wouldn't need a new husband, and Birdie and me won't have to have a different daddy. She could quit her job at Turner's Toppers and get in a better mood, which also means she'll get off Birdie's back because she'll be too busy laying around on hers eating bon-bons and reading *Photoplay* magazines.

If Mr. Yerkovich and his best friend, Mel, didn't need

any help around Bloomers, I could solve crimes and charge people. A lot of bad stuff goes on in this neighborhood, so that shouldn't be a problem, but if it is, I could also blackmail somebody.

After I'm in our bed at night and get done practicing singing and thinking about my TO-DO LIST and I still am not sleepy, I pull on a pair of shorts and a T-shirt and climb out our window when the weather isn't bad. I don't put on my sneakers so I can pretend to be an Indian while I walk around the neighborhood and look in windows and backyards and the insides of cars. People who sleep like rocks have no idea how much goes on at that time of night, more than you would ever imagine. I know all sorts of things that our neighbors would like to keep hush-hush for money. Like, after Mr. Lerner gets off the second shift from the Feelin' Good Cookie factory, instead of going straight home, he goes to Miss Peshong's house on Wednesday nights. I bet he'd pay me to keep my trap shut about how the two of them sit on the swing out back, eat those chocolate chip cookies, and neck each other while his wife is sawing logs in their bed. I'd feel half-bad about blackmailing Mr. Lerner because I really can't blame him for wanting to nibble on Miss Peshong, who is the other librarian at the Finney Library. The good-looking one. Not Mrs. Kambowski. She's a battle axe.

I try again to make Louise talk at the breakfast table by asking her, "Is there something wrong with your eggs?" because she hasn't touched them.

Like there are two stones tied around her neck, she lifts her head, takes a puff off her cigarette, drives the butt into the middle of the egg pile, and gives Birdie a snake look, hooded like that. This means she's unhappy with something that my sister is doing and that I better do something about it ASAP.

Since I'm not that nuts about Louise in the first place and almost everything that comes out of her mouth is bad news, I like it when she stops talking to us, but the silent treatment makes my sister's jitters worse. I press hard on the top of her leg. She's bouncing it against the table and making the food look as nervous as she is. Even worse, she's doing the most annoying bad habit that gets under our mother's skin. "You're humming," I tell her. "Knock it off."

Louise gives us a bad look, pushes her chair back, and before she leaves for the day, I say, "Please, please don't forget that Birdie . . . I mean, please don't forget that Robin Jean needs new shoes for school. She can't fit into her penny loafers anymore. Could you stop at Shuster's and pick up a pair on your way home from the hat shop? And two pairs of Wigwams? Please? She wears four and a half. Thank you very much. You look beautiful."

I think my imagination must be running away with me because Louise almost looks like she's gonna cry when she leaves the kitchen and heads straight out the front door. She didn't say no, so I hope that was a yes to the shoes, even though she hasn't gotten her first paycheck yet.

I tell my sister, "Okay. You can hum again, but not too loud." I need to listen for the roar of the woody heading down the street out the open kitchen window so I know for sure that Louise has, as Zorro would say, *vamanos*-ed. This is my favorite window to stick my head out of in the springtime because right below it is where the pink peonies blossom, and boy, oh, boy that smell is heavenly. Gammy told me that peonies stand for bashfulness, which I don't have, so I don't know why I love them so much. Lilacs are my second favorite. They smell terrific, and they're my favorite color.

When I can't hear the woody's muffler ratting against the street anymore, I push my chair back and tell Birdie, "Time to get the show on the road!" She's barefoot. She hasn't said anything, but I bet her sneakers don't fit her anymore either. "Get your socks and my old sneakers."

It didn't take me long to do the breakfast dishes because Birdie licked all the plates clean, so when she goes to our bedroom, I pull the bread out of the box and make us two oleo and sugar sandwiches because they're her favorite and the bread is fresh. Since she's ascared outta her wits to come with me to the graveyard today, I am making sure there are refreshments to keep her calm. She gets ~~jumpy~~ jumpier if there's no food in the vicinity. I wish I had something for dessert, but we can always swing past Mr. Linley's grave and pick up the box of chocolate-covered cherries that his lady friend leaves for him.

I'm working at the counter next to the sink, so I can't see Birdie when she comes back into the kitchen. "You almost set?" I ask.

"Like a table!"

"Birdie!!!" I drop the sandwich-cutting knife down on the counter and spin around. "You told a good joke!"

"I heard it on the *Rocky and Bullwinkle Show* yesterday," she says with a proud smile. I understand why Louise doesn't love me, but the Bird? How can she resist those dimples?

THE UNDERTAKING OF TESS

I can't help myself. When my sister looks at me so adorably, even though I'm trying to act strictly business, I stop pulling our picnic together, and give her a huge hug. She doesn't smell like herself—sweaty, and sweet like candy. Uh-oh.

"Honey?" I wonder if when she was licking the leftovers if she accidentally swallowed the L&M Louise stuck in the eggs. When we do the supper dishes, Birdie sometimes picks a butt off our mother's plate and puts it in her mouth so she can put her lips where her mom's have puckered up. I put my sister an arm's length away. "You didn't . . .?" But out of the corner of my eye I see that the orange filter rolled onto the floor next to the table leg, and that's a huge relief because Birdie *could* eat a butt. Almost nothing she would do would surprise me anymore. She's like a living, breathing *Gotcha!* (If he was still here, Daddy would be proud of her. A day doesn't go by that she doesn't scare the hell outta me, sometimes more than once.)

I crouch down, tie the laces on my old sneakers, and then I get back to slipping the sugar sandwiches into the brown paper bag. Looking for a grave is hard, hot work, so I grab two bottles of Graf's root beer out of the fridge and stick a church key in my shorts pocket. That makes me smile. (Daddy called bottle openers that because of the confessions everyone makes in the bar when they get soused, but that's not the only reason. He thought Pabst Blue Ribbon walked on water.)

I scrunch the top of the lunch bag down and ask Birdie, "You ready?"

"It's Freddy," she says with a giggle. "Let me in."

She shoulda quit when she was ahead. But as we jump down the back porch steps and run toward the black iron cemetery fence, I tell her, "Good one! Two for two!" With school starting tomorrow, the poor kid could use all the compliments she can get 'cause she's gonna get called "Bird brain," and probably "Pee brain," since I'm sure everybody in the neighborhood saw the white sheet with the yellow stain that Louise hung off our front porch.

Jump before You Fall!

I'm singing, "*Oh, what a beautiful morning, oh, what a beautiful day,*" when Birdie and me are running toward the cemetery fence, but that's just to keep her spirits up. No matter how many times I tell her that we have all day to look around for Daddy's pretend grave because Louise won't come home until after work, she's not buying it.

And now she's got *me* worried. If for some unknown reason, Louise didn't stay at the hat shop all day . . . Jesus H. Christ. That would be very bad. She might even have what is known as a nervous breakdown if she found us over here. Even though she is not a great mother, she's all we got except for Gammy and Boppa, who love us a lot, but are too old and sad to take us in after the men in the white coats haul Louise away.

I know a lot about this subject because Mrs. Brown down the street had a nervous breakdown. She did something so naughty and not nice that they shipped her off to a santatorium. She was on her front porch waving a butcher knife and yelling—I could hear her all the way down the block—"I didn't want to poison Scruffy! I had to! He was talking to me . . . telling me to cut Hardy's thing off in his sleep!" She got to come home from the santatorium after a month, so I see her and her thirteen kids hogging a whole pew during Mass every Sunday. She doesn't seem jollier to me, just sorta sleepy. (Jimmy Brown told me in confession line last week that he's still really mad at his mom. Not because she poisoned Scruffy, but because his father threw out all the sharp knives and now the whole family has to use spoons to cut their meat and that takes so long that he misses the first half of *The Honeymooners* when it's on.)

Because Birdie would really hate living in an orphanage if Louise has a nervous breakdown, I'm gonna ask Miss Peshong to look up how you can tell if someone is having one—other than poisoning your talking dog—in the *Encyclopaedia Britannica* the next time I'm at the library. I've been trying to get up there for a week now because they have this book called *Freaks of Nature* that looks really interesting, and the newest Nancy Drew, *The Secret of the Golden Pavilion*, looks great too. I also got some other questions that I've been wondering about that the pretty librarian should have the answers to. She knows the Dewey Decimal System and you gotta be smart to figure that damn thing out.

LIFE'S LITTLE MYSTERIES

1. Why does Nancy Drew have a friend who's a girl, but is named George?
2. How does Father Ted find all those Pauls?
3. Why did Daddy have to die?
4. Who is Charlie McCarthy?

5. Have you ever heard about anybody resurrecting besides Jesus?
6. Do you have any books about sisters who wet their beds?
7. What is a slut?
8. What is the fastest way to give someone hardening of the arteries?

I scurry over the cemetery fence and drop to the other side without a hitch, then I tell my sister through the black bars like I do every single damn time, "Stick your foot there, okay, now boost yourself up and don't forget to suck in your tummy." Maybe I shoulda made her wear her Playtex girdle today. "More."

Birdie makes it to the top after a couple of tries, but instead of listening to me when I tell her, like always, "Now swing your left leg over and make your way down," she stopped at the top. She's teetering.

"Jump before you fall on one of the points!" I say.

"I . . . I can't. I'm too ascared!'

"Quit being such a worry wart," I tell her after I shift into my Glinda, the Good Witch of the North voice because that's the nicest one I have. I'll pull out my Wicked Witch of the West one, though, if she doesn't start listening to me better. "Louise won't be home until five thirty. The church bells will let us know when it's time to head back." That doesn't work. She's still wobbling. I need something more powerful to talk her into disobeying our mother. "When we get the box of chocolate-covered cherries offa Mr. Lindley's grave, we don't have to share, you can have all of 'em!"

That does the trick. Candy almost always does.

Birdie licks her lips, and swings her other leg over, but instead of carefully sliding down, she yells, "Geronimo!" and goes sailing through the air and down to the ground like braveness came over her all of a sudden. I am not happy about this. What if her wild streak is coming out like when she sticks her head outta the car window or rings head-stuffing Mr. Johnson's doorbell?

I help her up off the ground and stare into her light eyes. They *are* a little too wide, so I point to one of the parts of the cemetery that I haven't scouted out yet and say, "Let's start searching over there," to remind her that we're here to find Daddy's pretend grave and not go weirder or wilder. As I hurry off in that direction, even though I'm the boss of us, I ask her if that's what she wants to do because she should get a vote, that's the American way. "S'awright?"

No answer. No laugh.

When I turn around to see why not, Birdie isn't shadowing me like she's supposed to. She's standing still and looking back at the black iron fence. Her lips are moving, and she's smiling her head off like she's talking to me, but she's not. Oh, no! Maybe that's why her eyes were so wide! It wasn't a streak coming over her, she's . . . she's going blind like . . . Helen Keller!

I trot back to her, hold up three fingers in her face, and say, "Count 'em." She does, so her eyes are working fine, so what the . . . ? Is she talking to *herself*? Like all crazy people do? If she does that in front of our mother. . . . I get ahold of her ear, just a little, and tell her in my Sister Raphael voice, "No talking to yourself. That's not allowed!"

She usually buckles right under when I use the nun's crotchety voice, but this time she swats my hand away and giggles. "I'm not talkin' to myself, silly," she says. "I'm talkin' to Bee."

"Talkin' out loud to bees is also not allowed. Same goes for flowers, rocks, houses, cemetery fences, and . . . and just about anything else but dogs, people, and God is not a good idea. I'm warning you, Bird." I get her by the shoulders and squeeze really hard. I hate to scare her like this, but a girl's gotta do what a girl's gotta do. "If you keep this up, they're gonna throw you in the snake pit."

She doesn't look terrified at all, which *really* surprises me. Birdie and me thought that *Snake Pit* movie was about boas and pythons falling into a hole before we saw it at the Tosa Theatre. It wasn't. It gave the both of us nightmares for months, and it still does if I think about it in the middle of the night. Going crazy is the biggest thing that I'm afraid of in all of life. Not spiders or rabid dogs or ghosts. You can squash a spider, shoot a foaming-at-the-mouth dog like they did in *Old Yeller*, and throw holy water on a ghost, but the crazy? Seems like it just sneaks into you and you can't do anything to stop it once it sets up shop in your brain.

Birdie shakes herself free from my hands and says a little too uppity for my taste, "For your information, I'm not talking to *bees*. I'm talking to . . . ," she spins around, "her." She is pointing at absolutely nothing. "Her real name is Betsy Elizabeth, but she said I can call her *Bee*. She's my new friend."

A Friend Indeed

Dreaming up a pal is not what Louise meant when she told Birdie and me that we should try to be more popular. This is more like, "Being between a hard place . . . between a hard rock . . . and. . . ." What the hell *is* that famous saying?

What am I supposed to say to Birdie? I can't let her know that seeing people that aren't there is also not good, that would really hurt her delicate feelings. How does something like this happen? Has she been hitting the bottle? Like that guy in another movie we saw who had a very tall, invisible bunny friend named Harvey? She begs me all the time to take her up to Lonnigan's. I don't, because I'm afraid that'll get back to Louise, but has Birdie been sneaking up to the bar without me the same way I been sneaking over the cemetery fence without her?

I take a step closer to get a whiff of her breath. It smells like cherry Pez and nothing like Daddy's after a long shift, so that's good, but it doesn't really solve the problem.

I ask her in a very ho-hum way, like this sort of thing happens every day, "So . . . ah . . . you and your friend are the Bird and the Bee?"

She nods and smiles from ear to ear.

I can't help it. The Bird and the Bee? That hits my funny bone. Even though I shouldn't encourage her, I tell my sister with a real, big laugh, "That's rich." Daddy would yuk it up if he was here too.

My baby sister doesn't know what that means because she's getting held back this year, so she won't go into fifth grade, which is where you learn that the birds and the bees has something to do with how babies are made. She doesn't know about "things" and "wieners" either, not the way I do. Kevin Remmington told me at recess last year when we were hanging out on top of the monkey bars together, "The man takes his wiener and puts it into the lady's bun and wiggles it all around. That's what it's all about."

That sounded like the hokey-pokey and not so bad until a picture of the Oscar Meyer Wienermobile came into my mind. (Heavens to Murgatroyd! Maybe *that's* why Scruffy kept telling Mrs. Brown to cut off Mr. Brown's thing. He was only trying to protect her!) Kevin Remmington started telling me more, but I fell off the monkey bars because I covered my ears. (That recess is also when I learned that knowledge doesn't always give you power like it says on the library sign. Sometimes knowing something makes you never want to eat a hot dog again as long as you live.)

A lot of stories like that go around school. You have to hear them even if you don't want to. We all know our mothers push us out of their tummies, but what we're not sure about is how we got in there in the first place and what that has to do with birds and bees. Plenty rumors about our teachers float around too. "They weren't born with boobies and that's how they know that they're supposed to grow up and be nuns," Marvin Howard told everyone because his father is the barber and he hears things. "And the nuns can't have babies even if they wanted to because after they sign up they get hung upside down in the bell tower and their holes are filled with cement by the Archbishop."

I ask Birdie as we walk past a few of the graves, "Does Bee . . . ah . . . talk back to you?"

"A course! She told me just now that you're crowding her and that you should move over and give her a little elbow room."

I take a giant step to the right. "What does she look like?"

Birdie studies the girl who isn't there. "She's got brown hair, and her eyes are Robin's egg blue like mine, and she's the exact same tallness as me, but . . . ," she looks closer, "she's prettier and skinnier and . . . she's really smart and her mother loves her a lot. She knows big words and can read like you, and she's very brave." She stops for a second, like she's listening to her friend tell her something. "And she can do magic too!"

Oh, boy.

I thought her and Bee just met today, but it sounds like they've known each other for awhile. How did I miss this? Maybe this is where she goes when she drifts off. She pays a visit to Bee. A chill runs up my spine when I wonder if Louise knows. I put my arm around Birdie's shoulder as we walk toward the graves across from the pond. I ask her in my most serious voice because this is no laughing matter, "You . . . ah . . . haven't told anyone else about

Bee have you?"

"Uh-uh."

Thank you, sweet Jesus, Mary, and Joseph! Thank you from the bottom of my wicked heart!

"Well," I tell Birdie with my best fake smile, "It's neat that you've got ah . . . new pal, but I think Bee should stay one of our sister secrets." We have a lot of 'em. Stuff that only her and me know from spying around the neighborhood, visiting the cemetery, and just plain keeping are ears to the ground. "Okay?"

She doesn't answer me 'cause she got distracted when we pass the grave of Dargu Malishewski—Born July 10, 1911 – Died April 22, 1957. It's one of Birdie's favorites because it's kept up really well and looks very peaceful, which is kinda funny considering how Mr. Malishewski died. According to Mr. McGinty, he got shot in his head in his taxicab outside the Greyhound Station by someone that took all his money and never got caught.

I would never do something like that to get rich, but seeing someone else murdering someone could be *really* helpful. If you don't tell the police on 'em, you could get a lot of dough to keep your mouth shut. But until my luck changes, here's my list of people who could be blackmailed for at least $50, or definitely $14.99, which is how much penny loafers and two pairs of Wigwams cost at Shuster's Shoes, plus the ten cents you put in the slot near the toes so you can use the pay phone in an emergency.

CRIMINAL ACTIVITY

1. Mrs. Holcomb steals apples from Mrs. Mertz's tree.
2. Arnie Esbach cheats in arithmetic from Patsy Johnson.
3. Miss Peshong and Mr. Lerner watch the submarine races in her backyard on Wednesday nights. I think that's a mortal sin, but maybe not. One of the Ten Commandments says that thou shalt not cover your neighbor's wife with kisses, but it doesn't say anything about covering your neighbor's *husband* with kisses.
4. Butch Seeback ties tin cans to the tails of the kitty cats his mother started selling after his father ran away with Vera Schmidt to Niagara Falls—chief exports: water and honeymoons. Butch also tried to kill one of those kitties. He put it in a gym bag and threw it in the cemetery pond late one night and ran away. I've got living, breath proof, *and* an eyewitness, so that makes it an open-and-shut case.

Number four would be the best blackmail! Butch is pretty dumb, so if I threatened to call the cops on him if he didn't give me some hush money, he wouldn't know that they'd probably decide that what he did to the kitty was attempted justifiable homicide. Once they did some digging around, they'd find out that Mrs. Seeback loves those cats a lot more than she does her kid. (Who could blame her?)

The reason it would be called "attempted justifiable

homicide" and not just plain "homicide" is because Mr. McGinty and me were firefly catching not far from the pond the night Butch threw the kitty in. You'd think hearing a bomb blow up almost on top of you would hurt your hearing, even make you deaf, but his shell-shocking did just the opposite. Mr. McGinty's hearing got super powerful, much better than mine, so he heard the splash, but my night vision is really good from being up at all hours and I saw Butch run away.

After Mr. McGinty jumped into the pond and rescued the poor little thing out of the sopping wet bag, I got a little nervous when I saw what unlucky color it was, but he told me that he wasn't superstitious, that the kitty was a boy, and that he was gonna keep him. He let me name him whatever I wanted to. I thought about it for a few days. 'Cause he's black, I figured we should call him Midnight after Buster Brown's cat, but then I decided we should call him Pyewacket after the cat in the *Bell, Book, and Candle* movie. (That Kim Novak, she's really something, prettier than Marilyn Monroe.) Pye lives in the shack with Mr. McGinty now. I strongly suspect that cat has some sort of magical powers just like his namesake. He looks at me all the time like if I don't pet him, he's gonna cast a spell on me, so I do, because he also looks like he could hold a grudge.

Once we're past her favorite grave, I tell Birdie, louder this time, "We gotta keep Bee a sister secret. That means,"—I really have to spell things out for her or she can get forgetful or get mixed up—"that you shouldn't mention her name in confession." The priests tell you that they won't tattle on you to your mother, but I don't believe them. "And don't tell the kids at school about the new friend you made either." That would be around the neighborhood in a flash. I almost told her, "And don't write about her in your how I spent my summer vacation story either," but since she can't write very good, I don't have to worry about that. "And whatever you do, you have to be really careful not to talk to Bee in front of Louise because. . . ." I can't tell her that this would be the straw that broke our mother's back, which is where her nerves are located. "She . . . ahhh—"

"I know, Tessie," Birdie says in her teeniest voice. "Bee already told me that Louise wouldn't let us play together anymore if she knew we were friends."

"She did?!" I can feel my jaw drop open. "Well . . . that's good, real good. Bee is not only very pretty, she sounds very smart." A lot smarter than my sister. Maybe this isn't gonna be as bad as I thought. This imaginary friend might turn out to be a real help in taking care of Birdie. Who cares if Bee's not really here? It's the thought that counts.

The two of us, well, I guess it's the three of us now, at least until Birdie moves onto something else weird that I get the chills just thinking about, don't stop to stare at Harriet Jones's grave because it always makes us feel sorry for her. If you hung out in a graveyard for as many years as we have, you'd know who is missed and who isn't too. You wouldn't be fooled by a big marble gravestone. Size doesn't matter. The real way you can tell if someone misses someone with all their heart is if they come to pull the weeds that Mr. McGinty misses, or if they stop by and leave the dead person, at the very least, a fresh tussie-mussie. These are darling little bouquets that Gammy taught me all about when we worked in her garden together. Tussie-mussies go all the way back to Merry Olde England times when people didn't use flowers just for smelling, but to send secret messages to other people. All flowers have special meanings. Like roses stand for romance and baby's breath for purity. When I find Daddy's pretend grave, I'll go to Mr. Yerkovich's flower shop and buy a purple gladiola to lay on it. Glads stand for remembering, and purple stands for "I'm sorry."

Birdie slows down at one of the fresher graves. They always give me an instant tummy ache because it makes me think about how the Grim Reaper can come get you whenever he feels like it. That dead person was here last week, probably eating bratwurst and having a gay old time, and now they're not. There are two yellow chrysanthemum plants that I bet were watered with tears because the Teddy Bear propped up against the stone looks damp. There are a ton of baby angels carved into the stone of poor:

Catherine Wilma Otis
Born January 1, 1948 – Died August 22, 1959
Beloved Daughter
Loved for All Eternity by Her Parents James and Dorothy

Birdie stops. "That's the grave of the coffin we saw getting buried the day of Daddy's pretend funeral when you painted my fingernails shell pink and I won six Candy Land games in a row."

How come she remembers all that, but seems to have

conveniently forgotten she lost a jinx to me that day? I haven't gotten a dime offa the little cheapskate.

"You sure that's the same grave?" I look behind me to see if I can see the back porch of our house through the leafy trees even though I know she's right because besides all the other great things about my sister, she has an excellent sense of direction. Birdie is my compass.

Cathy Otis must really be missed because there is also a whole bunch of white daisies resting in front of her stone. I pick one up and stick it in Birdie's hair with the bobby pin that's not holding back her too-long bangs, then I herd her over toward the pond because she gets very red in the cheeks when it's hot. She's got on her blue shorts, so I tell her, "Look at you! You look like the Fourth of July!" That makes her smile because that's her favorite holiday. She loves the parade that goes down North Avenue in the morning and the fireworks that get set off in Washington Park when it goes dark.

When we get in the shade of the willow tree that grows next to the pond, we strip off our socks and shoes and dangle our feet in the water. I try not to think about all the time Daddy and me spent here together. Since Birdie despises fishing so much, she doesn't have to remember that. She picks up a skimmer rock, flings it, then lies down on her back and chats with Bee about God only knows what. I can't make out what she's saying because she sounds like she does when she's praying.

"Okay, break time is over. We gotta get back to work," I roll over and tell her after the memories get too bad. "We'll look until the church bells ring twelve, then we can eat our lunch, and go get those chocolate-covered cherries off Mr. Lindley's grave." They've probably melted in this heat, but Birdie isn't fussy about the shape her chocolate is in.

We don't even bother putting our socks and sneakers back on because Mr. McGinty is an excellent lawn mower and the grass looks and feels like green shag carpet. I remind Birdie, "When we find Daddy, you gotta remember that it takes a little while for St. Peter to sort out the good from the bad things somebody did before he can open the Pearly Gates. So even though it's a pretend grave, like I told you before, the important part of Daddy will still be hanging around down there. I wouldn't be surprised if we saw some of his soul coming right out of the gravestone!"

Which it will. It'd be better if I could do this at night in the dark, that'd really be something, but beggars can't be choosers. I brought along our flashlight, and after we find him, at just the right minute when Birdie is bending down to kiss and hug the stone because she's so lovey-dovey, I'm gonna shine the Eveready on the back of the marble so rays'll come off it in beams the way they come offa saints in holy cards. She'll fall for that.

We're just coming around the corner of the Gilgood mausoleum, one of my all-time favorites because I really like the idea of being buried in a little house instead of underground where the worms will go in and out and turn my snout into sauerkraut. I'm not really looking very hard for Daddy's pretend grave because finding him in the fanciest section of the cemetery where the rich people are buried is a big waste of time. But today might be my last chance to find him and I can't leave any stone unturned and . . . HOLY COW! I rub my eyes, pinch myself, but . . . but two mounds down from the mausoleum . . . I'm so shocked that I can barely breathe or lift my arm up to point at:

Edward Alfred Finley
Rest in Peace
Born September 2, 1931 – Died August 1, 1959

I tell Birdie, who's looking in the direction of Mr. Lindley's grave and those chocolate-covered cherries, "Look! It's—"

But at that *exact* same second, Louise hollers off the back porch of our house, "Theresa Marie! Robin Jean!"

Goddamn it all! What's she doing home?

I'm Moving Her to the Top of My Shit List

Talk about bad timing!

Before Louise showed up, I was finally gonna get to cross #3 off my list:

TO-DO LIST

1. ~~Talk Mom into letting Birdie and me go to Daddy's pretend funeral.~~
2. ~~Convince Birdie that Daddy is really dead so Mom doesn't send her to the county insane asylum.~~
3. If #1 and #2 don't work out, find Daddy's pretend grave in the cemetery when Mom isn't around so Birdie can say goodbye to him once and for all because seeing really is believing. P.S. The resurrecting idea you had is a good one. Don't forget to tell her that.
4. ~~Decide if I should confess to the cops about murdering Daddy.~~

Louise can't know for sure that we're over here, she's just guessing. We could be anywhere. But it's such unbelievably rotten luck that she's calling for us at all that for a minute I think that I imagined her voice coming offa the back porch. I turn around to ask Birdie if she heard it too, but I can see that she did because she's turned into a white statue. But then all of a sudden, she topples down to the dirt because hearing Louise's yelling voice can drain the blood outta her face and cut her off at the knees.

I grab her under the armpits and drag her behind the mausoleum. Once I have her propped against the wall with my arm I bit by bit peek out. Parts of Louise appear and disappear when the breeze rustles the branches of the leafy trees.

I'm not sure if Birdie and me should hole up where we are, or take off as fast as we can in the opposite direction, but whatever we do, we gotta do it ASAP! I don't think Louise would climb the fence and come after us because her gray skirt is too tight to swing her leg over, but if she's having one of her tempers because she came home and found us gone and the house a mess . . . there's no telling what that moody woman would do.

"Robin Jean!" Louise shouts louder. That was foxy of her to leave me out of it. She knows that Birdie will answer her before I ever would.

"Oh, Tessie, oh, no," my sister slobber-pants on my arm.

"*Shhh.* We . . . we . . . you gotta. . . ."

I look over at Daddy's grave hoping that seeing it will knock sense back into me the same way I was hoping it would knock sense into Birdie, which I still think it will once she sees it, when outta the blue, I get the funniest feeling that he *knows* that we found him and that he's playing a *Gotcha!* joke and Louise is in on it. Is . . . is that possible? Supposedly, all things are, but I just don't know anymore. My brain that's usually so quick and sharp feels like it's exploding inside my skull. Like I stepped on a land mind the same way Mr. McGinty did and all my smart ideas are blowing up into a million little pieces. Should I laugh? Cry? Tell my sister, "Eureka!" because we finally found Daddy's grave, or should I rush over to Mr. McGinty's shack and thank him over and over for pulling some strings so our poor daddy's pretend grave could be in the ritziest part of Holy Cross, or . . . or maybe I should just pick up Birdie's hand and we should run away to join the freak show at the Wisconsin State Fair, or just keep going all the way to Oklahoma?

The only thing I know for sure is that I wanted this to be a happy-ending day for Birdie, a big celebration, and here she is hiding next to me, sweating, shaking, and letting me know in her tiny voice that I let her down. "You told me we could get the chocolate-covered cherries off Mr. Linley's grave and I could eat them all."

She tries to stand up like she's gonna head over there, but I yank her arm hard, put her face in my hands, and make sure she's looking deep into the windows of my soul when I tell her, "I'm sorry, I forgot." I could kick myself for not picking up that box of Stover's off his grave first thing. I could use it right about now. Candy *always* makes her less jumpy. "We'll get them later. I promise."

I try to slow my thinking down the way I do when I play checkers with Mr. McGinty, who I beat all the time. What should Birdie and me do? We should . . . we should . . . wait until we see what Louise's next move is before we can know what our next move should be. Yes!

I lean my back against the mausoleum, close my eyes, and rub Daddy's Swiss Army knife really hard. When a few minutes go by without a peep from Louise, I think it worked and our luck took a turn for the better, so I'm just about to grab Birdie's hand and make a run for it when our mother shouts from the back porch like she knows for sure that we're over here and was just waiting for us to let our guard down, "Girls? Time to finish up what you're doing and come home!"

Huh.

Now that I'm over the shock of first finding Daddy, and then Louise showing up to ruin the surprise for Birdie, I'm thinking clearer. And what I'm thinking is that something's fishy. I know all our mother's voices by heart and this isn't her goddamn-it-all-I'm-going-to-give-you-a-spanking-that-you'll-never-forget one. It might be her get-in-the-car-I'm-going-to-drop-you-off-somewhere-and-not-come-back-for-three-hours one, but it doesn't really sound like that either. Louise sounds sorta . . . excited? Happy?

Birdie must hear that in her voice too, because she's stopped making that kitten mewling noise and is taking in a deep breath like she's gonna shout back to Louise, "Hello! We've over in the cemetery looking for Daddy's grave. Be right there!"

But I know how foxy Louise is. She could just be pretending to sound happy, so I quickly slap my hand over my sister's mouth and tell her in my Edward G. Robinson you-dirty-rat voice, "Zip it, or I'll zip it for you, sister," then I slowly stick my head out from the side of the mausoleum to get a better gander at our mother. I wish I already had that pair of binoculars I've been saving up for because if I could only see her face clearer, I'd know in a jiff if she's trying to pull a double cross. Her right eyebrow would be arched.

Birdie peels back one of my fingers and whispers, "What's she doin'?"

"She's turning around and . . . ," thank you, Saints Peter, Paul, and Mary, "she's going back into the house."

When we hear the screen door slam shut, I let out the breath that I didn't even know I was holding and tell Birdie, "Quick. Stick your socks in your pocket, get your shoes on, and run!"

We don't climb into our backyard, or into Mrs. Klement's either, that would be dumb. We hoist ourselves over the part of the cemetery fence that's behind Charlie Garfield's house that's two down from ours. I always climb fast, but Birdie sets a new world record because there are worse things in life than getting impaled on one of those black points. There's Louise.

"Hi," bald Charlie says surprised when he sees us. He's sitting out in the backyard whittling because that's *his* main hobby. He can only make slide whistles and straight snakes because he's not good with curves yet. I told "Cue Ball" Garfield that he should try making pool sticks too, which he really liked the sound of, so I think he's gonna give that a shot. His other hobby is watching birds, so when I finally save up enough to get those binoculars, I'll let him borrow them whenever he wants. "Whatcha two doin'?"

I can't slow down to explain, no time for that. I point to his whittling knife, make the pirate cutthroat sign across my neck, and hold my finger up to my lips so he knows that we're up to no good, and then Birdie and me peel past him, through the side yard of his house, and out to the sidewalk.

We are bent over at our waists and panting like two rabid dogs. We gotta catch our breaths, and look presentable before we go home. I take the scab- and sweat-wiping Kleenex out of my pocket, mop Birdie up, do the same to myself, and say, "I'm gonna tell her a made-up story, so when we get in the house, let me do all the talking." I grab another breath. "No matter what, even if she's nice to you, keep quiet." My sister falls for our mother's tricks all the time. One kind word is all it takes. "Just smile with a lot of dimple and nod your head at whatever I tell her."

I reach down and grab four black-eyed Susans out of the garden in the front of our next-door neighbor's house. That's a nice little revenge on Gert Klement who I've decided to move to the top of MY SHIT LIST after we get home, if Louise doesn't beat us to death. I have really had it with that old lady. Every other day this summer, she's said something mean about me to my mother. "You better keep your eye on Theresa, dear. The girl is a ticking time bomb. Did you notice that she was laughing in the Holy Communion line on Sunday?"

MY SHIT LIST

1. Mrs. Gertrude Klement.
1. ~~Dennis Patrick.~~
2. The greasy man who tries to peek in the gas station

THE UNDERTAKING OF TESS

bathroom window when you gotta stop to pee because you can't make it home from the Tosa Theatre after you drink a large root beer.

3. ~~Mom.~~ Louise.
4. Jenny Radtke.
5. Mr. Dalinsky.

After Birdie and me kiss the St. Nick medal around my neck, I remind her, "Dimple-smiling, no talking." I spit on my hand and stick it toward her. "Promise."

She makes a loogie on her palm, gives my hand a hard, wiry shake, and says, "All for one, one for all!"

I have no idea where she came up with that.

I rub Daddy's knife one last time, and I'm so desperate that I even say a prayer. *Please . . . please . . . please don't let Birdie blow this. Just this one time.*

We take our front porch steps two at a time. Just to be safe, I check again that we look good. I spin Birdie around, and sure enough, she's got cemetery dirt on her butt leftover from when she turned into a white statue and timbered to the ground. I swipe it off, pull open the screen door, and begin to pretend that I don't know that our mother is home. She's not in sight, so she's probably in her bedroom sitting in front of her vanity mirror.

I squeeze Birdie's hand hard to remind her of the spit promise, and say real loud as we take baby steps through the living room, "It was such a good idea to put on your beautiful new Playtex birthday girdle and use some of our piggy-bank money to go up to Bloomers and buy Louise flowers to thank her for working her fingers to the bone for us at that horrible hat shop! You're so smart, Birdie. If only Mr. Yerkovich hadn'ta been in such a hurry because he was working on that big wedding, he coulda wrapped them up in that nice pink paper. His poor floppy wrists. We should pray for him."

The whole time I'm saying that malarkey, I'm pointing like crazy at the living room wall and acting like I'm Louise putting on lipstick on the other side of it so Birdie'll know that's where she is.

"Ya know what we should do?" I say to my sister, again very loud. "We should go up to the attic after we clean the house super-duper good. We could look for some tissue paper to wrap the flowers in and—"

"*Gotcha!*" our mother yells when she jumps out of the hallway outside her bedroom.

Neither one of us saw this coming. Birdie screams and so do I. "We . . . we . . . holy shi—I mean, holey moley . . . that was a good one!" I tell Louise. "*Ha . . . ha . . . ha.* We were gonna surprise you and . . . and you surprised us instead!" No joke. "You really got us!" I laugh again, and then my sister does too. Mine is fake, but hers is high pitched and I have to elbow her to stop.

"Oh, are these for me?" Louise acts like a blushing bride when Birdie shoves the black-eyed Susans I ripped outta Mrs. Klement's garden her way. "My favorites! Thank you, Robin Jean." She tilts her head to one side and looks closer at my sister. She is looking at her hair and narrowing her eyes, so I do too. Damn it. The flower I stuck in Birdie's hair at the cemetery is still fastened to the bobby pin holding back her bangs. How did I miss that? Louise flicks it with her pointer finger and asks, "Did Mr. Yerkovich put this in—?"

"Yeah, he sure did," I jump in and say before Birdie can blurt out that we got the daisy from a bouquet that was on the grave of little girl named Cathy. "Hey . . . how come you're back so early from work? You look really beautiful. Did the hat shop burn down?"

When Louise's laughs, I'm surprised it's so regular sounding. I thought it would sound more like a rusty gate at a haunted house 'cause I can't remember her using it since Daddy died. "No, the shop didn't burn down," she says with a very sly smile. "Something even better happened!"

She probably got fired. Now I'll have to borrow some money from Mr. McGinty, or pick someone off my list and blackmail them tonight, or we won't be able to buy school lunch tomorrow. Birdie can't go long without eating.

"*What* happened?" I ask Louise.

"The woody had a flat tire on the way to work this morning and I had to pull into the Clark station to have it checked and . . . I met a man! We're going out to dinner and a movie tonight!" She looks down at the watch that Daddy gave her for Christmas. "I better start getting ready!" She rushes toward her bedroom singing, "*Love and marriage, love and marriage go together like a horse and carriage.*"

Oh, boy.

Looks like if our mother has her way, which she always does, she's gonna spend the whole afternoon making herself irresistible so she can lure the greasy guy who works at the Clark station into her feminine-wiles trap.

I wonder if after she marries him if Birdie and me are

gonna have to stop calling him "The Peeker" and start calling him Daddy.

It's Either a Sign from God or Clark

"So? What do you think?" the lovely Louise asks Birdie and me after we spent hours cleaning the house. I let Birdie talk to her imaginary friend the whole time because our mother would think she was talking to me, but after she called us into her bedroom, I made my sister promise again that she wouldn't say a word to, or about, Bee, or our visit to the cemetery or Daddy's pretend grave or Gammy and Boppa or Mr. McGinty or Mrs. Turner or anything or anybody else that would make Louise have one of her 100% Irish temper tantrums. Birdie said, "Okay, Tessie," but that and a dime will get you a cup of coffee because face it, she is not a good accomplice. She's too sweet and honest.

We're not usually allowed on ~~their~~ her bed, so Louise must be in a really good mood over this date. I'm lying on my back on Daddy's side. Birdie is on her tummy with her head in her hands looking at our mother like she really is a movie star. She tells her with a sigh and stars in her eyes, "You look prettier than . . . than . . . Ida Lupino."

"She means Maureen O'Hara," I say fast because my sister forgot how much Louise despises Ida Lupino for some unknown reason.

Didn't matter really. Louise didn't hear Birdie's compliment. She's too busy admiring herself in the full-length mirror on the back of the bedroom door.

"Fix TV dinners for supper," she says to me. "Take an extra good bath, scrub out the tub with Dutch cleanser, lay out your uniforms for school tomorrow, and then go straight to bed." She didn't buy Birdie new penny loafers at Shuster's Shoes today. I guess she got too excited about finding the man named Leon Gallagher to marry at the Clark station. According to her, he's *not* the greasy guy I was worried about, and she might be right, because "The Peeker's" real name isn't Leon, it's Gordon, it says so on the front of his uniform.

Louise clips her gold earrings on her lobes and says, "Leon's the one, girls. Mr. Right." She crosses herself. "Getting that flat tire had to be a sign from God."

I'm about to say, "Or Clark," but Birdie cuts me off when she asks, "Does he look like Prince Charming?"

Louise closes her eyes, like there's a picture of the guy on her eyelids. "He's a little too thin, but I'll fatten him up."

I am already feeling a little sorry for the poor man. If he's skinny now, he'll waste away to nothing if he has to count on Louise's cooking. Maybe that's all part of her foxy plan. Marry him, make sure he puts her in his will, and then starve him to death.

"Leon . . . Mr. Gallagher's feet and hands are small, but he's handsome in other ways, except for his melting jaw line." Louise spins around and checks the back of the emerald-green dress with the black bow. She really is a breathtaking glamour puss. "And I've been saving the best news for last." She bends down and adjusts the seam on her stockings. "I was so upset that I might have to buy a new tire after it went flat that I let it slip that I couldn't afford one because I have two mouths to feed and guess what he said?"

"I have a melting jaw line. You got two mouths. Nobody's perfect," I say snotty-like.

Louise darts her eyes my way and says, "Watch the wisecracks, young lady," but then, because she likes what she sees in the mirror and her future, she gets happy again. "Actually," she says, "Mr. Gallagher told me that he likes kids, especially little girls. The more the merrier."

Hmmm. "The Peeker" has small hands and feet and he likes little girls, the more the merrier too. Maybe he was wearing a disguise and going by the alias Leon this morning.

"Are you *sure* he's not the really greasy guy who works at the station?" I ask Louise.

She shoots me one of her dagger looks. "Leon is well-groomed, and he was only pumping gas today because the regular guy didn't show up and the owner, who's a friend of his, asked him to help out." She picks up her can of Aqua Net off her vanity and gives her hair that is flowing down in perfect waves past her shoulders an extra spritz. "He has a very good job on the American Motors assembly line. You know what *that* means?"

It means that I don't have to get a job at the flower shop or blackmail anybody or look for rainbows with pots of gold sitting at the end of them, but it also means exactly what I tell her, "Mr. Gallagher is the answer to your prayers."

Louise licks her lips with the tip of her tongue and smiles like a cat. It's an excellent imitation of Pye right before he swallows a trapped mouse. "God helps those who help themselves, Theresa," she says. "You'd do well to remember that."

Ohhh, don't worry your pretty little head about that, Louise. Not a day goes by that I don't remember that.

Sure, I was upset at first when she told us about the fella she met because Birdie and me don't want another daddy, but maybe her meeting Mr. Gallagher really is like Louise said—a sign from God. There *is* that famous saying, "He works in mysterious ways."

We have that in common.

I spent the whole time Birdie and me were cleaning this afternoon coming up with a plan that's better than any Nancy Drew caper.

When Louise goes out the door on her date tonight, Birdie and me are gonna head back to Daddy's grave so she can finally say goodbye to him. After she recovers from all her joy, I'll mention that resurrecting idea to her, and then we'll come home, take our baths, scrub the tub with Dutch cleanser, lay out our uniforms, and crawl between the sheets the way Louise told us to. We'll spoon, and I'll plant lavender on Birdie's back, and then I'll FINALLY cross #3 off my TO-DO LIST. That'll make me feel like I really *did* do a good deed, which might help me to not feel so bad about murdering Daddy. Maybe I'll even fall asleep tonight feeling not proud of myself because it's a sin to let your head get swollen up, but, oh, I don't know . . . maybe I'll feel like I didn't throw in the towel.

When a car horn makes an *ah . . . oo . . . ga* sound out

front, Louise grabs her clutch with the lipstick and compact that she dropped inside. She dabs a little extra Evening in Paris on her wrists and gets an even bigger cat smile and an arched right eyebrow. She's got something up her sleeve. "I'm paying Mrs. Klement to keep an eye on you tonight, Theresa, so don't think you can pull any of your shenanigans."

Goddamn it, she's foxy.

Now Birdie and me are going have to wait until after it gets dark to pay our visit to the cemetery. And instead of using the backdoor, we're gonna have to leave by the basement window on the other side of the house that buttinski Mrs. Klement can't see from hers. This is gonna throw a monkey wrench into my plan because I love going over to the graveyard at night, but Birdie? She's terrified of the dark.

When Louise's bed starts bouncing beneath me, I look over at my sister. She's gotten up off her tummy and is jumping up and down. Uh-oh, just like I suspected earlier, she's about to go wild-streaking. It looks like—I yell, "Birdie, NO!"—but I'm too late. She launches herself off the bed, flies through the air, and practically lands on top of Louise.

God, I don't know what gets into her sometimes! She knows our mother doesn't like to be touched, but especially, after she's all done up. She's got Louise around the waist and is burying her adorable face in the folds of the green dress.

Birdie says muffled, "You're more beautiful even than . . . than . . . Ida Lupino."

"Oh, for crissakes," Louise says as I pry my sister offa

121

her. She swipes her hand down the front of her dress, checks to make sure that Birdie didn't leave any stickiness on her backside, and is about to say something not nice when the sound of the *ah . . . oo . . . ga* horn comes through the bedroom window again.

"You better get going," I say, very sincerely.

She checks her face one more time, says, "Lights out at nine," and is almost out the front door to land herself a new man and us a new daddy when she stops, turns around, and shakes her finger in my face. "Behave yourself, Theresa. I'll give you and your sister the lickings of your life if I hear from Mrs. Klement that you left the house."

After she was done reading me the riot act, she turned on her high heels and disappeared through the front screen door. Birdie calls out to Louise as she sways toward the red car waiting for her at the curb, "We'll do just what you told us to. And we promise to stay in the house. Cross our hearts and hope to die! I love you!" She presses her little ski-jump nose against the screen door and watches as Louise gets in the car, then she says to me in a softer voice, "That's what we'll do, okay, Tessie? No shenanigans."

I hate lying to her, so I cross my fingers behind my back before I make my eyebrows go up and down, pretend I'm smoking a cigar, and say in my very good Groucho voice that I know will make her laugh because she really loves that show, "You bet your life, little lady."

All Your Dreams Can Come True

After I make Birdie and me the fried chicken, mashed potatoes, corn, and brownie frozen dinner for supper the way Louise told me to, we don't sit down and dig in at the yellow kitchen table. We take the silver trays into the living room and eat in front of the television set.

From across the way, I can feel Mrs. Klement's beady eyes boring into my head like an outer space ray, but I refuse to look at her. She thinks she got the best of me. I'd choke on my chicken if I saw an I-beat-you-at-your-own-game look on her face.

The only thing on TV is the news. They're talking about Hawaii becoming a state again. Chief exports: pineapples and hula skirts and lepers. I get a little closer to the set because I don't want to miss seeing some lepers because I am really interested in them. But all that comes up on the screen is a picture of something the newsman calls a *loo ow*. That must be what people who live in Hawaii call a party that they have on a very nice-looking beach. Everyone is wearing flowers around their necks and some dark-skinned ladies are making their hips shake around a pig with an apple in its mouth.

When Birdie and me finish eating our supper, I turn the

set off. She wants to know, "What shoes am I gonna wear to school tomorrow? Mine are all worn out." And they give her blisters, but she doesn't care about that. She just wants to look sharp. That's very important to her. That's another thing she musta inherited from Louise.

I dust off the brownie crumbs from her mouth, pinch the X's she made with the string, swoop them down the middle, and tell her, "I'm gonna stuff some newspaper into my loafers from two years ago. They'll be fine for tomorrow, just don't do lots of running at recess. I'll remind Louise at breakfast to pick new ones up after her job."

After Birdie beats me in nine rounds of cat's cradle, we play cards, her other specialty. Go fish and war. Everything I'm doing is about making her feel good. First food, and then these games that she always wins. The happier she is, the less afraid she'll be to disobey our mother and go into the cemetery at night.

When the streetlights finally pop on, that means it's almost time to do my plan. I can't ignore Mrs. Klement anymore the way I have been. I need to sneakily check out the living room window every few minutes to see if she's still watching us. Her house is so close that I can see the black hairs growing outta of her ugly, pointy chin. She had her window open so she could try and hear what Birdie and me were talking about, but I closed ours so she couldn't. I want to pull the curtains shut so bad, this would make everything so much easier, but if I do, she'll report that to Louise, so all I can do for now is grin and bear Gert.

I jump up off the plaid sofa, point to the clock that's on

top of the coffee table, and tell Birdie, "Oh, look at the time! Ya know what's on right now? *Walt Disney Presents!*" This is her favorite show because she would very much like to live in "The Magic Kingdom." Maybe *that's* where we'll go when we run away. "We missed most of it, but I bet you can catch the last part. I'll do the dishes by myself, so don't worry about that."

Birdie claps her hands and says, "Thank you, Tessie! It's Bee's favorite show too! Hurray!"

It takes some time for the picture tube to warm up again, but after it does, and I find the right channel, Birdie and Bee get cozy, and I clear our dishes off the TV trays and take them into the kitchen. This is a smart move. This is what Indians do when they're being followed. They split up so their enemy doesn't know who to go after.

Mrs. Klement can only see me in the kitchen if she cranks her neck really hard because that side of her house only has a small, high window that she has to use a stool to see out of. The reason I know what the inside of her house looks like is because I wait for her to go to the Red Owl on Thursdays when they give out the S&H Green Stamps, and then I push open her back hallway window that she can't lock anymore because I jimmied it too many times with a screwdriver.

When I crawl through the window of Gert's house, sometimes I take the change off her bedroom bureau to buy candy for Birdie, but mostly I just move stuff around. I'll hide a frying pan in her bed, or stick a toilet brush in her refrigerator, or change the hands on her clock because I'm trying to give her hardening of the arteries, which is what happens to old people instead of going crazy. I got the idea to play tricks on her brain after Birdie and me saw the *Gaslight* movie at the Tosa Theatre. Since cramping my style is her biggest hobby, I don't feel bad at all about doing the same to her. Two days ago, the old poop had the nerve to tell Louise that she thought Mr. McGinty might be "too friendly" with me. What a crock. Everybody knows that a person can't be too friendly, so maybe my tricks are finally paying off.

In a way, I'm doing good for two other people too, because it's not only *my* life that will be so much better when Gert goes off to the old folks' home. She has a granddaughter named Lily who is so nice that I think the old witch must've bought her from gypsies. Lily drives all the way from downtown to spend every Sunday with Gert. The reason she has so much time on her hands is because she's not married. Not because she's ugly, she isn't. She's got a darling ducktail and a pretty figure and she dresses very cool. She told me once that she has a hard time meeting men because she's very busy at her nursing job. So once Gert is out of the way? Lily will have every Sunday free to go on a date, and I got an idea who she could do that with.

I check the clock above our stove. Splitting up from Birdie, who's still watching the TV, will only buy me a little time. Gert would never stay in her living room looking at my sister looking at the Walt Disney show for very long. She knows I'm the ringleader. She'll come after me, but it will take her some time to pull the stool up to the window to watch what I'm up to because she's got bad knees.

I take the laundry pen out of the mess drawer in the

kitchen to make a sign that I'm going to hold up to the living room window after I go back to be with Birdie. I write on the inside of the box the TV dinner came in.

We're taking our long baths now and then going to bed. Sweet dreams!

That stinks. The first part is good, but that last part is too nice. That would make somebody who calls me, "The hellion," suspicious. I fix it.

We're taking our long baths now and then going to bed. ~~Sweet dreams!~~ So why don't you go sit on a screwdriver and rotate?

That's much, much better. After I hold the sign up so she can see it, I'll take it with me and leave it at the cemetery, that way when Mrs. Klement tells Louise tomorrow that I told her to screw herself, I can tell her, "What's she talkin' about? Sign? What sign?" Then I'll put my hands on my cheeks and get a real hopeless look on my face. "Maybe you should call Lily to come and enroll her in the old folks' home ASAP!"

"Tessie?" Birdie calls from the living room. "It's over!"

I put the laundry pen back in the drawer, rinse the mashed potatoes off our forks, run into our bedroom to get my flashlight, and hurry to her.

When I plop down on the sofa, she puts her head on

my shoulder and says sorta dreamy, "Should we start our baths now like Louise said?" because that Disney show can do that to her.

I answer, "I need you to do a favor for me first." The reason I haven't told her yet that I spotted Daddy's pretend grave this afternoon is because I want it to be a surprise. A wonderful *Gotcha!* that she'll never forget. "Remember when we were at the cemetery today?"

She shivers. "That was a close call."

"Yeah, it's good Louise didn't catch us, but . . . ," I put on my saddest face, "something else really bad happened when we were over there."

Birdie gets up on her knees and says, "I know. We didn't get the chocolate-covered cherries."

"Yeah, that was bad, but . . . something even worse."

"Oh, no, what?" she says like she can't imagine anything worse than not getting the box of Stover's off Mr. Lindley's grave.

"Daddy's Swiss Army knife musta fallen outta my pocket when we were hiding from Louise behind the Gilgood mausoleum." She knows that I *have* to have his knife. I can't live without it, and I can't sleep AT ALL unless it's under my pillow with my lists. "I gotta go back and get it."

Birdie's sad face is better than mine because hers is real. "But it's nighttime, and Louise told us to stay in the house . . . no shenanigans."

Since I knew the dark would be a problem, I am more prepared than a Boy Scout. I pull the flashlight outta my shorts pocket and say, "But what about Daddy's Swiss Army knife, Bird? What if somebody finds it and keeps it and . . . and we never see it again? I couldn't stand it if. . . ."

I can fake cry, make real tears and everything, so that's what I do, because as much as she's ascared of our mother and the dark, she goes to pieces when I put my face in my hands and sob. It's for her own good. And mine. I gotta cross out #3 on my list.

I peek out at Birdie between my fingers. She looks confused. I get worried for a second that she might say, "You go find Daddy's knife and I'll run our bath water," but she throws her skinny little arms around me and says, "A course, I'll go with you, Tessie. Please don't cry."

I wipe my tears off with the back of my hand, snivel a little, and tell her, "Thank you, tweetheart. We'll be quick, I promise."

She looks over at the house next door. "But what about Mrs. Klement? She'll see us leave out the backdoor. What're you gonna tell her?"

"She won't see us. We're going out the basement window. And I'm not gonna *tell* her anything. I'm gonna stick this up in the window." I pull the sign that I made in the kitchen out from behind my back. Birdie can't read it, so I tell her that it says what I originally wrote before I made it better, "We're taking our long baths now and then going to bed. Sweet dreams!"

Birdie makes her amazed mouth. "Tessie, that's so smart. Bee thinks so too!"

I am beginning to like this imaginary friend more and more every second.

A Maybe Miracle

After I hold up the sign in our living room window, I don't even wait to see how Gert reacts. I grab Birdie and we rush down the back steps into the basement. She won't crawl out the window until I swipe the dead flies off the sill, but then she does great.

When we come out on the side of the house that Gert can't see, I think to myself that luck might be on our side tonight. Even if our nosey neighbor figured out that we weren't taking our baths and hurried to check for us out her kitchen window, between the darkness, and Birdie and me wearing our black shorts and T-shirts, she wouldn't be able to see us. And there aren't any stars or a moon to light us up tonight either. I can smell rain in the air, and from far off, thunder booms. Daddy loved storms.

Birdie and me get over the cemetery fence much easier than usual too, so things are really going smoothly. I'm leading the way and admiring the cemetery. It's even more beautiful to me at night. Everyone tucked in and surrounded by all the love and flowers and presents that the people who miss them leave on their graves. It's quiet, except for the frogs croaking at the pond, and a lightning fork in the sky that makes Birdie say, "I'm hungry."

I thought of this.

"I brought you my brownie from dinner." When I take it outta my pocket, I'm very careful not to let the Swiss Army knife *really* slip out.

I decided not to tell Birdie the resurrecting idea because I had too many other ideas to work on, so I crossed it off my TO-DO LIST. Just finding Daddy's pretend grave will have to be good enough for tonight. When we come around the corner of the mausoleum, I'm gonna throw his knife on the ground, bend over to pick it up, then pretend to notice his gravestone for the first time. "Birdie! Look!" I'll say. "Eureka!" and then I'll race ahead of her and shine the flashlight on the back of his gravestone so by the time she gets there it will be so believable that his soul is shining through.

When we get closer to the mausoleum, I say, "What the Sam Hill . . . ?!"

I have never, ever seen this many fireflies. There's a swarm of them lighting up this whole part of the cemetery.

Birdie laughs, claps her hands, and is the happiest I have seen her in the longest time. "Bee says she called the fireflies to show us the way to Daddy." She stops and listens to what her imaginary friend is telling her. "He's right over there." She points two graves down from the Gilgood mausoleum, which is exactly where he is.

Holy Jehoshaphat! This . . . this is better than Our Lady appearing to the kids at Fatima!

Or else Birdie and me really have gone off our rockers.

When the lightning cracks right above our heads, I jump almost outta my skin, but usually nervous Birdie doesn't even seem to notice. She's gone ahead without me and is almost to Daddy's grave.

"Wait . . . wait for me," I shout, and hurry to catch up.

I fumble with my flashlight so I can light up his stone the way I was planning to so she thinks his soul is coming out of it, but when I get up next to her, I don't have to. There already *is* a beautiful, golden light shimmering out of the grave of:

Edward Alfred Finley
Rest in Peace
Born September 2, 1931 – Died August 1, 1959

The light grows and grows and rises up to surround Birdie and me.

My sister laughs, hugs and kisses the gravestone, and says, "Hi, Daddy. It's me and Tessie! Hello! Hello!"

We tell him what's been going on since he's been gone—the same way other visitors do when they come by to talk to their dearly departed—until we're almost washed away by the pouring-down rain. Birdie, with the shimmering golden grave light all around her and the lightning cracking across the sky and the wind forcing the trees to bend at their waists, stands up and says, like she's the boss instead of me, "Tessie and me gotta go now Daddy before we get electrocuted, but we'll come back and see you soon," then she grabs my hand and we slosh toward the cemetery fence.

I boost Birdie over first, and when it's my turn to climb, the sign that I made for Mrs. Klement that I shoved down in my shorts pokes me in the back. I gotta get rid of it so there's no evidence that she can use against me. I stop at the top of the fence, hold up the sign, and let the wind rip it outta my fingers.

I'm not sure how long we've been gone, but I think longer than we shoulda been. The lights are still out in the house, so Louise hasn't come home from her date yet. Even if she was standing out on the back porch waiting for us, Birdie and me would gladly follow her into the house and take whatever stupid punishment she'd come up with because what happened to us at the cemetery? I don't know what the hell it was—a maybe miracle . . . a mirage . . . or something that kids see when they lose all their marbles—all I know is nothing that Louise could do would make us sorry about tonight.

Birdie and me are smiling like crazy at each other while we take our baths, towel each other off, scrub the tub, lay out our uniforms, put on our nighties, and slip under the sheet. We haven't talked too much about what we saw. I think because that famous saying, "Seeing is believing," really *is* true. We're lying in the dark, holding hands, breathing, and listening to the rain beating against our bedroom window.

Birdie says, "Tessie?"

"Yeah?"

"I know ya keep telling me that I gotta stop being so weird or I'll end up in a snake pit, but when that golden light came outta Daddy's grave tonight—"

"Uh-huh."

"Did it feel to you like one of his hugs that he'd give us before he tucked us in and said, 'I love you two as much as the stars and the moon?'"

I was about to ask her the same thing, but wasn't sure

if I should. What if she hadn't felt it? That would've hurt her delicate feelings. "Yeah, Bird. It felt *exactly* like one of his hugs."

"Okay. Night, Tessie."

"Night, Bird. Night Bee."

After she falls asleep faster than usual, which I didn't think was possible, I take our flashlight, the ballpoint pen, and my list out from under my pillow, and cross out #3:

TO-DO LIST

1. ~~Talk Mom into letting Birdie and me go to Daddy's pretend funeral.~~
2. ~~Convince Birdie that Daddy is really dead so Mom doesn't send her to the county insane asylum.~~
3. ~~If #1 and #2 don't work out, find Daddy's pretend grave in the cemetery when Mom isn't around so Birdie can say goodbye to him once and for all because seeing really is believing. P.S. The resurrecting idea is a good one. Don't forget to tell her that.~~
4. ~~Decide if I should confess to the cops about murdering Daddy.~~

Even though tonight was really something, when I get the chance, I might eventually tell Birdie about the other idea I had, because if she can have an imaginary friend who can call a million fireflies to light up a pretend grave with golden light, and if Daddy can reach down from Heaven to give us a hug that is making his two girls feel cherished forever . . . I guess resurrecting would be possible too.

I crumple up my old list and get busy on my new one. I can never be without one. That'd make me feel too much like Birdie, like a drifting love boat. Someone's got to be the captain of our ship.

TO-DO LIST

1. Pick up the *Freaks of Nature* and the new Nancy Drew at the Finney Library.
2. Think faster.
3. Steal a sun lamp from Dalinsky's Drugs to use for grilling people.
4. Sell more potholders to make money for the binoculars from the *Superman* comic, or blackmail someone.
5. Tell Father Ted in confession that you murdered Daddy, but use Mrs. Klement's voice because her artery hardening is taking too long.
6. After her grandmother gets sent to the Big House, set Lily up on a date with Mr. McGinty.
7. Ride the Schwinn to Meurer's Bakery after school tomorrow and buy three cupcakes that Birdie and me can take over to the cemetery and eat with Daddy on his birthday on Saturday. Get his favorite, yellow with chocolate frosting.
8. Practice for Miss America.

I slide the new list under my pillow, switch off the flashlight, and sing *My Favorite Things*, until I remember that I gotta set the alarm for 5 a.m. in case I have to take our sheet down to the washing machine. But just when I'm bending over her to do that, I stop. I bet none of those people in the Bible that were lost but got found wet *their* beds, so now that we found Daddy, Birdie probably won't either.

As long as Louise doesn't end up accidentally marrying "The Peeker." If she does, then all bets are off.

ACKNOWLEDGMENTS

To the generous souls who shared their love, support, and expertise—thank you, thank you, thank you.

My family: My eternally loved son, Riley, whose kindred spirit never leaves my side. Casey, my best friend, daughter, and hero. Our all-around good egg, John-Michael. Heaven-sent little ones, Charlie William and Hadley Ann Orion, who inspire us with their *joie de vivre* and flat-out hilariousness.

Crystal Patriarche, and the entire team at SparkPress: Many thanks for making publishing a truly exciting, respectful, and cooperative effort.

Editor, Wayne Parrish, who is brilliant and gentle, and shared wonderful insights.

My literary agent, Kim Witherspoon: Your belief in me never ceases to amaze. I'm honored to be represented by Inkwell Management.

The James E. and Rebecca Winner Foundation for the Arts that so graciously supports my efforts.

My fellow writers, early readers, and wonderful hand-holders: Sandy Kring, Bonnie Shimko, Beth Hoffman, and Dr. Meagan Harris.

And to you, dear reader: I can only hope that the Finley

sisters touch your hearts as much as your continued support and encouragement throughout the years has touched mine.

From *New York Times* bestselling author
LESLEY KAGEN
comes the poignant and unforgettable continuing story of
the Finley sisters in,

The Resurrection of Tess Blessing

Available December 2014 at a bookstore near you.

An excerpt follows. . . .

While Others Leave Her Side, I Never Will

My Tess is a sly one. Quite the little actress. When called upon to do so, she can appear to be a concerned citizen . . . a capable mother . . . the confident wife of the president of the Chamber of Commerce. Appearing ordinary is one of her best talents. As long as nothing unexpected blows up in her face, which, of course, life being the minefield that it is, is about to.

Morning winter sun is streaming through the four-paned kitchen windows that overlook the white picket-fenced backyard of the darling redbrick colonial in Ruby Falls, Wisconsin, population, 5,623. There are three of us gathered around the distressed pine kitchen table that's been passed down through the Blessing family for generations—forty-nine-year-old, Tess, her lovely eighteen-year-old daughter, Haddie, who has returned to the roost to spend the Christmas holiday, and me, who has always been and always will be, but remains unnamed, for the time being. The man of the house, Will, has already left for the day. He's busy seating the breakfast bunch at Count Your Blessings, the popular Main Street '50s-style diner that he inherited from his father upon his passing. Tess's other child, Henry, a junior in high school, remains upstairs wrapped in his *Star Wars* sheets. Like most fifteen-year-olds, the boy believes the world revolves around him.

"Just a nibble?" Tess asks her daughter.

When the gifted photographer struggling through her first year at Savannah College of Art and Design turns her nose up at the French toast her desperate mother prepared with her secret ingredient—tears, Tess can barely keep herself from pounding the top of the pine table and asking yet again, "What did I do wrong? How can I make this better? Please . . . please let me in." She swallows the questions back because she knows from experience that Haddie'll only change the subject, at best. Worse, she'll get angrier than she already is.

Tess sets her gaze out of one of the kitchen windows and locks on the solitary snow angel I watched her create last night while her family remained snug in their beds. Others may leave her side, but I never have, and never will. We are bound together not only in this life, but for all time.

Most of what you think you know about "imaginary

friends" is probably inaccurate. We're a much more complicated lot than the way we're often portrayed in books, movies, psychological articles, and such. For instance, not once have I heard it mentioned what an important part readiness plays in our relationship. Nor have I seen it noted how we are imbued with whatever qualities our friends need the most, which depends upon at what point in their lives we are called into what is known on our side as, "Service." The profound spiritual component in our friendship has never been touched upon either. Even the term, "imaginary friend," is nothing more than a handy phrase a psychiatrist came up with to describe the indescribable and put the inexplicable in its place.

Since Tess has had quite a bit of prior experience with an IF—a nickname we like to call each other sometimes— I'm not anticipating that she'll put up much of a fuss when the time comes for us to connect again. *(At Last.)* While I can't know exactly when that momentous occasion will occur—that's entirely up to her—I can feel it drawing nearer. Hoped it might happen last night when I was perched on the faded green Adirondack chair under the weeping willow tree in the Blessings' backyard watching her swish her arms and legs back and forth in the snow. (Wearing just her ancient cows-sipping-*café-au-lait-on-the-Champs-Élysées* nightie on the chilliest night yet this winter proved that she needs someone to lean on sooner rather than later.)

Because I know every thought and feeling she's ever had, as Tess sets the French toast Haddie had rejected on the floor next to the family's beloved golden retriever,

Garbo, I can hear her telling herself—I'm gonna do it again tonight. Not just once, I'll make a dozen angels.

And on January 17, 1999, after the dawn smudges peach and blue across tomorrow's horizon, she'll rise from her bed, slip on her worn-to-the-nub green chenille robe, and pad downstairs to get things going in the kitchen like her world hasn't cracked wide open and the contents spilled. And before Haddie takes off for an eight-mile run, Tess'll wish her a perky good morning, offer her a cup of freshly squeezed orange juice, and not mention the life-shattering news she's about to receive. My friend will put on the smile she keeps close at hand, point out the kitchen window at her newly created flock, and say, "Look! Angels have come by to say halo!" with the hope that her daughter will be tickled by the corny joke she'd thought was hilarious when was she was ten 'cause Tess would do and say just about anything to recapture the closeness of those days.

Angel shmangels. How many times did I tell you not to have children, Theresa? Yours barely speak to you and look what they did to your figure and. . . .

If you're thinking that's me talking mean like that to Tess, well, you'd be wrong.

That there is the unrelenting voice of her mother that she hears in her head even though the gal's dead.

When Louise Mary Fitzgerald Finley Gallagher passed on last year, instead of leaving her eldest daughter a 1940s bureau with a couple of missing porcelain handles or linen hankies with swirling lavender initials, she left Tess her remains, a heart full of pain, and her head full of criticism.

I'm not sure where Louise is in her celestial education

at the current time—upon the death of her body, her soul moved from the living room to the school room where she will be held accountable for her actions and be given the opportunity to learn from her mistakes—but while she was still on Earth that self-centered woman did indelible damage to my friend that I hope to heal when she allows me in. I have a couple of ideas on how to remove her thorny mother from her side, but have yet to come up with anything to stick in the hole to staunch the bleeding. (Not yet, anyway.)

Tess sets the washed fry pan on the yellow-and-blue kitchen counter, wipes her hands dry on the seat of the bulky, gray sweatpants she wears to conceal the blubber she's put on in her efforts to show Haddie how much fun eating can be, checks the clock above the stove, and looks for the black purse that holds her good-luck totems—a hanging-by-a-thread copy of *To Kill a Mockingbird*, remnants of her children's baby blankets, and her daddy's Swiss Army knife that fell out of his pocket that fateful day on the boat. She doesn't go anywhere without that lucky purse.

"I've got an appointment this morning," she tells the girl whose photographs are so remarkable for one so young that *National Geographic* has shown interest in hiring her as an intern next summer. "Why don't you call me when you're done shooting at the Nature Center? Maybe we could—"

"What kind of appointment?"

"No big deal. Just my yearly mammogram."

"Does it hurt?"

Tess lays her cheek atop her daughter's head and

breathes deeply. Her natural aroma has always been earthy. Like she'd grown the child not in her womb, but her garden. Haddie's hair is really something too. Not a deep red like her mother's, but a daisy yellow like Will's used to be, and the child was blessed with eyes that are a paler shade of blue than Tess's that are almost navy. "Nothin' to worry about, honey," she reassures. "Cancer doesn't run in the family. Mammograms are just part of the program when you get to be—"

"Uh-huh," her daughter says as she ducks away from her mom's lips.

My friend has been raked over these coals so often that she's grown used to and accepts the rejection, but that doesn't mean she doesn't try everything she can to change it. She's sure that if she could only figure out *why* Haddie is so angry with her, she would get better and they could go back to the way they used to be. Inseparable.

Tess wonders if it's because of the way she reacted when she was first informed that her daughter planned to attend college at the Savannah School of Art and Design. Was that it?

She can't deny that she was far from thrilled that Haddie meant to fly off and leave her in her contrail. When the acceptance letter was waved in her face, Tess freely admits she said, "Georgia?" like it was the one on the Black Sea. (She also failed to hide the excruciating ripping sensation she was feeling that was not dissimilar to the eighteen-hour back labor she'd endured during the child's birth.)

But . . . once she'd gotten over the shock, hadn't she tried her hardest to be supportive of Haddie's desire to test her wings the year before she left?

Unfortunately, due to the losses she had experienced as child, the profound sense of abandonment Tess was experiencing was almost impossible to contain. Even though she's normally highly skilled at keeping her true emotions secret—she's successfully hidden her severe emotional problems from her children and the rest of the world her whole life—it was pretty damn obvious that she didn't mean it when she threw kisses and hollered, "Go get 'em, baby!" on the mid-August afternoon that her husband and daughter pulled out of the driveway in the packed-to-the-roof green Taurus her parents had given their overachieving, artistic child after she'd graduated with the highest grade-point average ever recorded at Ruby Falls High.

So, of course, when the homesick freshman called begging to return home sixteen days after her arrival in Savannah—"Mommy, please . . . I made a mistake. I miss you . . . I'll eat whatever you want. Please, please come get me," Tess didn't think twice. She scribbled a late-night "Be Back Soon, xoxo" note to Will and Henry, and off she and Garbo drove to save Haddie from her freedom.

She made it as far as Zionsville, Indiana, when the doubts she'd been wrestling with forced her to pull into an abandoned truck stop. Under the fluorescent lights, she finally admitted to herself that as much as she wanted to bring her girl back home, if she did, she'd be acting as selfishly as her own mother had. She cried herself dry, and then called Haddie to tell her in a barely used firm voice that she was sorry, but, "You need to stick it out."

Is that why she's mad? Tess wonders. She thinks I

wasn't there for her when she needed me most? She takes another stab at connecting with Haddie before she leaves for her appointment. "Maybe we could get a little lunch today?" In the good old days, shrimp egg rolls followed by chicken chow mein used to be her daughter's favorite. The number-four special would be out of the question, but maybe she could talk Haddie, who appeared to know the caloric content of every food ever created, into a lettuce wrap. "Wong Fat's?"

On her daughter's generous lips even disgust looks good.

What did you expect? Louise snipes in Tess's head. You just invited a kid with an eating disorder to lunch at a place that has FAT in its name. Theresa . . . Theresa . . . Theresa . . . could you be a worse mother?

I wish my friend could shout back, *Yeah, I could be you!* but at the present time, she doesn't have the confidence to speak back to her mother, nor bury her either.

Tess tries again. "Do you want to . . . ?" She almost asked Haddie if she'd like to go to the mall instead. That would've been another mistake. Her girl used to adore shopping, but she won't try on flouncy dresses or frilly blouses anymore. She'd grab armfuls of pretty things off the racks, but once they hung in the dressing room, she would collapse in tears after she stripped down to her panties and saw her "grossness" reflected back in the store mirror. "What about . . . ?" Haddie adores illness movies. If she could find one about a young woman suffering with anorexia or bulimia she'd be in hog heaven and expect her mother to wallow in it with her. "We could watch a

Lifetime movie tonight."

"Whatever."

Sensing that she's hit yet another conversational dead end, Tess clears the rest of the breakfast dishes and slogs down the basement steps to turn off the TV that Will and Henry left on last night. When she steps back into the kitchen with her arms full of their leftovers, Haddie shudders at the greasy popcorn bowl, empty pop bottles, and gooey candy wrappers.

"Thanks for rubbing it in," she growls as she stomps past her mother toward the staircase.

Tess calls after her, "I'm sorry . . . I'm stopping at the grocery store after my appointment. Do you need anything?" but she leaves the house uncertain if Haddie heard her before she slammed the bathroom door shut behind her.

ALSO BY LESLEY KAGEN

The Resurrection of Tess Blessing

Whistling in the Dark

Land of a Hundred Wonders

Tomorrow River

Good Graces

Mare's Nest

ABOUT SPARKPRESS

SparkPress is an independent boutique publisher delivering high-quality, entertaining, and engaging content that enhances readers' lives, with a special focus on female-driven work. We are proud of our catalog of both fiction and nonfiction titles, featuring authors who represent a wide array of genres, as well as our established, industry-wide reputation for innovative, creative, results-driven success in working with authors. SparkPress, a BookSparks imprint, is a division of SparkPoint Studio, LLC.

To learn more, visit us at sparkpointstudio.com.

CPSIA information can be obtained at www.ICGtesting.com
Printed in the USA
BVOW08s1558250815

414963BV00004B/76/P